THE WITNESSES ARE GONE

JOEL LANE

THE WITNESSES ARE GONE

Influx Press
London

Published by Influx Press
The Greenhouse
49 Green Lanes, London, N16 9BU
www.influxpress.com / @InfluxPress

This edition 2023.
Printed and bound in the UK by TJ Books.
First published in the UK in 2009 by PS Publishing
Paperback ISBN: 9781910312971
Ebook ISBN: 9781910312988

Cover design: Vince Haig
Interior design: Vince Haig
Proofreader: Dan Coxon

For Tindal Street Fiction Group – the last gang in town

THE ABSENT AUTEUR: AN INTRODUCTION TO *THE WITNESSES ARE GONE*

M. JOHN HARRISON

'The world's in crisis and you're living in a dead industrial district, watching films about madness.'

Joel Lane's first collection of short stories, *The Earth Wire*, was the kind of book you hear about from other people. Within a year of borrowing a copy from someone and not returning it, I had lost three further copies, bought and paid for, by lending them to people who didn't return it. It's a quiet measure of an author when someone recommends you a book they borrowed from someone else you lent it to, a circular signal-pumping process that everyone ought to be glad to take part in; sometimes there were more degrees of separation than you expected, sometimes rather fewer.

That was in the early-to-mid 90s. I was down on my luck and couch-surfing Harringay. It seemed like exactly the right place to be reading *The Earth Wire* if you weren't living in the industrial Midlands of the UK. The fact is, reading those stories was exactly like losing concentration on the towpath of some disused Black Country canal and scraping your bike along a brick wall on your way home in the dark. It had that same heart-stopping quality, the sudden lively twist of the handlebars, the over-correction, the dirty water that, previously beside you, now lies in front. You wonder about someone who can give you that sensation.

Later, I met him, around London, mostly at strange wrenched evenings at Filthy's, where we would stand in corners drinking quietly, too shy to say much to each other listening to other writers read their stuff. Joel was, you sensed, as hard on himself as his characters, out of some bleakness, some idea about the world that wasn't going to be revealed: the result being a quality often found in horror stories – the sense of a symbolic structure which doesn't quite let the reader in on its real themes, instead guiding you to where you can make a leap of your own. It's a genre technique that, broadened away from genre, led to and still drives the best of what's now called 'the Weird'. It's also a kind of demand, challenging the reader to dig into their interpretive reserves, to examine not the fiction so much as themselves. Twenty eight years later Joel's no longer with us, but that characteristic challenge of his resides, haunting this 2009 novella.

The Witnesses Are Gone begins in a familiar landscape, a familiar climate both actual and economic, on a deserted Midlands railway station where infrequent goods trains rush past filled with 'new cars, toxic waste or nothing at all'; makes its way via chains of badly made and managed websites to a real-life contact in the Thames Estuary; and ends unilluminated by the 'dense grainy sunlight' of Mexico. In between these mismatched nodes of experience, it visits Paris and somewhere that might be called 'beyond Paris', and takes a moody retrospective interlude in a kind of drowned Dorset, where the air is 'lukewarm and brackish, as if it had a mild fever'. In a sense it takes place in none of these locations, rather in the psychic landscape generated when narrator Martin Swan, after finding four mangled videotapes among the rubbish in his new house, enters the umwelt of cult auteur 'Jean Rien' and his mysterious contribution to the 'cinema of the unconscious', *L'eclipse des sens*.

What do we learn about Rien? Hard to say. He's that French art-house guy whose name, although you never quite remember it, rings a bell. Didn't he make one or two 'offbeat' horror films in black and white? Don't you associate him vaguely with Lucile Hadžihalilović? You skimmed an article on him a decade ago, in some old paper magazine, perhaps *Screen Bizarre*, years ago – it was already barely legible due to damp? As for the film itself—

Shot with heavy filters to create 'a sense of enclosed, rain-blurred twilight', it features a group of young people in a house. You watch them drinking, dancing, fucking. There's a room at the back that's always locked. 'From scene to scene, the occupants seem 'to undergo some kind of progressive sensory disorder'; later, obviously, the door opens, to reveal 'a darkness in which something like a child was crawling'. The tape is in such poor condition, Swan soon can't remember what he struggled so hard to see; a few days' later he's lost it anyway. 'It was more depressing than shocking,' he tells the members of his film group. We wonder instantly: does the film even exist? Can it even exist, under the terms and conditions Joel Lane now lays down, as Swan sets out on his increasingly obsessive attempt to retrieve the film, the film maker, the film's relationship to the world?

Not only Rien's work but Rien himself, he discovers, was a hoax: films circulating as *L'eclipse des sens* are further hoaxes, fan work, tributes to a nonexistent original. Other films claiming to have been made by Rien; interviews with him; articles about him: all hoax or rumour, all fading away as you investigate them. Under this kind of logic it's impossible to construct a working hermeneutics. Nothing you can know about *L'eclipse des sens* or its auteur is dependable. Worse, no way of gaining knowledge of *L'eclipse des sens* or its auteur is dependable. Rien is just that: Rien. Nothing gets you nothing. Nothing, anyway, beyond your mounting sense of instability and alienation.

Reality itself is no different, Swan is forced to conclude. Written and rewritten on a daily basis, it ends up 'thin and transparent, like a strip of celluloid'. People, too: 'Maybe I'm not really a person,' one of his early informants tells him, suggesting that a close encounter with Rien really will get you nowhere. Every life under capital – and especially any record or remains of it – is a solutionless mystery, a flickering, briefly separate world, a nagging epistemological problem for those who come after. 'Fantasy and deprivation always go together.' Every story is a story of ghosts. Every story consists in the author's attempt to enchant the reader, while the reader becomes more and more desperate to erase the author and receive the fiction as untold: that is, as real.

Don't forget to read the Acknowledgements, where the origin story of this story of Joel's reveals itself, or claims to.

ONE

Maybe if I hadn't bought the house, I wouldn't have found the videos and none of this would have happened. Judith would still be alive, and I'd have lost nothing except some memories I could live without. But I'm not convinced. I think it would just have found another way of happening. Even before it all started, I felt like I was living backwards. The future seemed more real than the past.

The house was in Tyseley, an industrial district on the south side of Birmingham. I moved there because I needed to be on the train line for my job in Warwick. The station was a bittersweet reminder of the days of adequate public transport: a beautiful, sombre Victorian building visited by more trainspotters than trains. Three of the four waiting-rooms were permanently closed. The toilets, which had an authentic scrolled iron screen in place of a door, were boarded up. Only the local trains stopped there, and not many of them.

My strongest memories of Tyseley are of waiting on the platform, watching the factories further down the line add their smoke to the clouds. In January the snow was grey, a sublimate of polluted rain. You'd know when a train was coming from the vibrations, just too low in pitch to be heard. Nine times out of ten it would be a freight train: dozens of jolting carriages, filled with new cars or toxic waste or nothing at all, going by so fast you had to turn away not to feel its wind on your face.

I was thirty-nine when I bought the house, and I suppose it had to do with needing to belong somewhere. It was a district in transition from industry to retail: new shops and wholesale outlets selling what local factories had once made – furniture, tools, carpets. I need to feel that I was in transition too, even if I couldn't say what to or what from. At the same age, Robert Smith had sung that he had *nothing left to burn*. I didn't feel burnt out, but I had a sense of time moving too fast. A certain nostalgia for the days when 'text' was a noun rather than a verb. After twenty years of rented rooms, I had the chance to unpack all my boxes and survey all the pieces of my life: books, letters, records, souvenirs. Maybe I can be forgiven for assuming that the pieces would fit together into some kind of meaningful pattern.

Another reason for the house was that I hoped Judith would move in with me. We'd been seeing each other for two years, staying at each other's flats, even going on holiday together a couple of times. But somehow the house didn't appeal to her. An Edwardian terrace with no central heating wasn't her idea of comfort. Maybe it reminded her of the run-down terrace we'd rented for a rain-dogged week in Dorset, our first summer together. Or it brought back memories of her five-year marriage to a paranoid civil servant in Walsall. Whatever the reason, being in the house any longer than a night depressed her. 'You wanted to make a new start,' she told me, 'but all you've done is hide in the past. There's nothing new here.'

The irony was that I'd never felt so close to her as when we were in the house. Her tension excited me: I wanted to touch her whenever she passed by. In my mind, she was the house's natural occupant. Her touch drew me into her private world: it gave me access to her memories, the rhythm of her breath, the dreams she hid behind open eyes.

The one thing Judith enjoyed doing in the house was watching films or videos on TV, curled up with me on the Afghan rug in front of the gas fire, drinking red wine. She liked thrillers, science fiction, anything that took her out of herself. Apart from booze she disliked drugs, which helped to stop me falling back into bad habits. We watched the entire second season of *Angel* on video, the broadcast version having been cut to ribbons by Channel 4. 'It's the potential for darkness that makes him so attractive,' she told me. 'Without that, he'd just be another pretty face. And if the darkness took over, you wouldn't go near him. Know what I mean?'

The creations of Joss Whedon certainly offered more insight into the nature of evil than anything issuing from the mouth of George W. Bush. It was a strange time. You had a president who'd corrupted an election talking about threats to democracy. And Britain fighting in a war against a country that was unable to defend itself. We were told to be on our guard against 'terrorist reprisals'. It wasn't terrorism when US planes bombed a wedding party, or when they wiped out an entire village as a gesture of frustration because Bin Laden had slipped through their hands. But it would be terrorism if the enemy did that to us. Despite the anti-war meetings and demos we attended, Judith and I both felt a sense of frozen helplessness. It was as if ordinary people no longer existed.

TWO

In March of that year, I decided to get the garden into some kind of shape. There were bushes to trim, weeds to pull, a damaged fence to straighten. I bought some gardening tools and cleaned out the shed. The previous owner had left several dead pot plants and boxes of rubbish; from their age and dampness, I suspected that she'd inherited them from the owner before. Newspapers twelve years old; paintbrushes whose bristles snapped when you touched them; densely printed books on railway history, the pages blotched and sticking at the edges. A cardboard box tore apart when I lifted it, dropping four black unmarked video cases at my feet. I wiped them clean and took them inside.

Judith was working that weekend, a freelance design contract. Her absence, as usual, left me feeling empty. I took a can of beer out of the fridge and sat down to watch the videos. The first was taped over with news broadcasts from the early nineties: the Gulf War, John Major, the Balkan conflict, the rise of Le Pen. The second was a series of history programmes from BBC2's Open University service, including a study of film newsreels and their representation of the news. The third video was a blurred nth-generation copy of two German hardcore porn films, the poor quality of the images attaching ectoplasm to the flesh and filling the mouths and other holes with a ragged darkness.

The fourth video contained a French art-film, with subtitles rendered illegible by a fault in the copy that distorted the bottom edge of each frame. It was called *L'éclipse des sens*, and directed by Jean Rien. I thought his name rang a bell, but I wasn't sure. I'd seen a lot of French films at the Arts Lab, before it became the Triangle Cinema, before it became a derelict building. This could have been one of them.

It was shot in black and white, with heavy filters used to create a sense of enclosed, rain-blurred twilight. A group of four young people, maybe students, living in a house. You saw them drinking together, dancing to old records; two went upstairs to make love, while one painted a shadowy landscape on a canvas and the other knelt on a balcony, praying to the night. There was a room at the back of the house that was always locked up.

The rest of the film was mostly a series of repetitions of that night. I wasn't always sure whether the scenes had been re-shot with variations or just touched up. From scene to scene, the occupants of the house seemed to undergo some kind of progressive sensory disorder. One boy played the piano, but his girlfriend heard only a kind of discordant screaming. The other girl looked in the mirror and saw a bruised, deformed figure. In one extraordinary scene, the couple made love frantically (and without apparent relief) in the garden while the other two walked slowly around them, either not seeing or not caring. Their blank faces scarred by rain. The painting developed over time to resemble a giant eye closing, with trees for lashes. Condensation filmed the windows, and damp began to streak the painted walls.

The later scenes had a religious feel. The piano player searched obsessively through a leather-bound book full of indecipherable, rune-like script. Hints of daylight and birdsong flickered to life, then faded. The records were played over and over, but the music had become a kind of deep choral lament with no tune, like the wailing of the damned. Yet the four never gave up dancing. The artist left his canvas, where the sun was eclipsed by a grey twilight, and started praying and chanting outside the locked door. Eventually he collapsed, lying in a foetal position on the filthy carpet. The door opened to reveal a darkness in which something like a child was crawling. The camera tracked slowly around the house: a cracked mirror, a horribly scratched record, a window coated with grease. A bed covered in fragments of plaster from a ruined ceiling.

There were no credits, or they hadn't been taped. I watched the blank screen for a minute or so, then switched the video off and ejected the cassette. The film hadn't really appealed to me, but I felt like it was trying to tell me something I needed to understand. Or perhaps it was just that I'd heard something about the director and couldn't remember it. Had I read an interview with him? The confusion depressed me. I cooked myself a fry-up while listening to *Songs From a Room*, a record Judith hated. The flat's colours seemed unreal after the film. I thought of the

7

solar eclipse in 2000, when Judith and I had stood at the lookout point on the Lickey Hills and seen night fall briefly onto the city. I was surprised by the sudden chill.

Later, I turned the spare room upside-down trying to find a box of film magazines. There'd been an article on Jean Rien; I remembered it clearly now. Some murky stills from his films, which were all in black and white. He'd made several offbeat horror films in France, one in rural Scotland and one in Mexico. The journalist had commented that copies of Rien's films had a tendency to disappear; he'd even tried to explain why, though I couldn't recall his theory. After emptying countless boxes, I found the magazines in an old briefcase. Damp had got into the leather, and the pages felt thick and greasy to the touch. Two issues of *Screen Bizarre* were stuck between issues of a 1970s porn magazine that I'd evidently considered worth keeping.

The article was largely converted to wordless pulp by some kind of paper-rot that had soaked into the magazine's spine. I could only read the title: 'The Enigma of Jean Rien' by W. Padgett. The damp made the photographs still more blotchy and shapeless than they would have been. At the bottom of the next page, I could just make out the words:

> ...and be forgotten, as if they revealed some entity that wanted to disguise its own existence. The last film was...

I tried to turn the page, but it tore in my hand and the yellowed paper disintegrated. The room smelt like a second-hand bookshop.

By now, a sense of dislocated time was adding to my loneliness. I managed to lose the rotting paper smell in a few glasses of whisky, then went to bed and tried to think of Judith. But her image kept blurring into the shadowy, misshapen figure of the girl in the mirror. At two a.m. I went back into the spare room, shivering, to retrieve the old porn magazines. It's come to something when even your masturbation fantasies rely on memorabilia. Like trying to call on a younger self to keep your need alive. Afterwards, I lay in the dark and told myself that the magazines falling apart meant they had no hold over me. The brittle photographs were no more important than the film.

THREE

Judith phoned me in midweek, a bit drunk. It was after midnight. 'I've just been to a CND meeting,' she said. 'Went to the pub after. Did you know that a train carrying nuclear waste runs through Tyseley? It's every other Sunday at four a.m. For all we know it could stop in Birmingham for hours. What if it crashed? We need to organise a protest.'

'What, a demo at four in the morning?' I tried to imagine a moonlit vigil, watching a freight train whose wooden carriages leaked a faint green light. 'There'll be no one there. I'm sure the signals are electronically controlled.'

'Saturday night, then. Give the youngsters coming back from the pub something to think about.' Alcohol often filled Judith with a kind of defiant idealism, a sense of transformation being a part of human nature. If she'd been drunk all the time, she could have joined the SWP. Sober, she chipped away at ideals until they collapsed.

'I saw a very strange film about youngsters at the weekend,' I said. 'They were locked up in a house, going mad. Some kind of entity was controlling them. A child that lived in the dark.'

'Sounds like a typical family. You know I hate that shit. Films should liberate the imagination, not choke it with misery.' She paused. I was about to ask her if she wanted to go out for dinner on Friday when she said: 'You know, I'm sure I've seen that film. Ages ago. Who's it by?'

Suddenly I drew a blank. 'Can't remember. I'm tired. Some French director. Jean Rien, that's it.'

'Means nothing to me.' She paused, then laughed. The sound had something painful in it. I got the point too late to join in. 'Why did you buy the house?' she said quietly. 'The world's in crisis and you're living in a dead industrial district, watching films about madness.'

'Do you want to go to the Casa Paco on Friday?' I asked. Judith in this kind of mood always made me tie myself in knots, but the best I could manage was a half-hitch.

'Yeah, okay.' Judith wasn't keen on European cinema, but she liked European food. Not that she was anti-intellectual. She just had to believe in the purpose of everything. Without that, she felt trapped in a kind of sick passivity. An endless rain.

I don't usually remember my dreams, but a few nights later I dreamt something I had little chance of forgetting. I was fourteen, and at some kind of school camp. We were learning how to sail. The first morning, there was a communal shower. Girls walked past me naked, lifting their towels and smiling. Suddenly aroused, I rushed to cover myself – then slipped on the wet floor and broke my ankle.

I was in hospital all day. There was a rainstorm outside; the sky went black. The news reached us that most of the kids had drowned.

When the first casualties were brought in, all I could do was watch. They were hardly recognisable: hair clogged with mud, clothes filthy, faces bloated and streaked with black weeds. Some of them were still alive, struggling to breathe, vomiting watery slime. None of them survived in the end. I lay there surrounded by girls I had wanted to touch. Their thin bodies were contorted by pain and rigor mortis. I could smell the black water that had poisoned them, hear it dripping from the trolleys and beds. Eventually I closed my eyes and curled up, playing dead.

I woke up crying. In the half-light, the dull functional objects of my bedroom made me think of an institution. Judith stirred behind me. There was a tension in her slow breathing, as if the air was too thin. I wanted to hold her but couldn't, even when she woke up. Somehow, I was sure she'd know what I'd been dreaming and feel betrayed.

———————

The Black Lodge was a group of SF and horror fans that used to meet once a month in an old pub in Hockley. Still does, for all I know. Judith and I went along a few times. The group, mostly in their thirties, had a healthy cynicism unusual in fandom. One of them, Ray Broadmoor, was better known as Ray Mondo: the film columnist for the magazine *City of Night*. If anyone could tell me about Jean Rien, he could.

But the whole group looked blank when I described *L'éclipse des sens*. 'Sounds like an amateur film,' Ann commented. 'Don't suppose there was a BBFC certificate on it?' I couldn't remember seeing one. 'Maybe it was banned on video, and that's why no one has seen it?'

Steve shook his head. 'It's not on the list of banned videos, I'm sure. And from what you're saying, it didn't contain much to put it there.'

'It was more depressing than shocking,' I said. 'There was a kind of hopelessness about it.' Already I couldn't recall a single scene with any clarity. Perhaps Rien's films just weren't memorable.

Ray tapped his forehead with a knuckle. 'I think I've seen something else of his,' he said. 'A few years ago, at a festival of underground films in Leeds. It was about three a.m. and I'd had a few pints, so it was all a bit of a blur. Something about an icon, a hunched thing with black teeth and empty eye-sockets, that ruled a village. You kept seeing it in mirrors and pools, but never directly. There was water everywhere. Streams of light, heavy filters on the camera.' He looked uneasy about remembering so much.

I got the next round in. When I returned to the table, the conversation had moved on to the disappointing second series of *Urban Gothic*. Later, Ray and I were standing at adjacent urinals; I didn't observe whether his lager produced paler urine than my real ale, but it wouldn't have surprised me. The mention of Jean Rien had evidently stuck in his mind, since he asked me, 'Have you talked to Barry at the Electric? That old hermit's seen every film shown in Birmingham since 1970. He makes Kim Newman look like a beginner. He's not a great horror fan, though. But maybe we're not talking horror at all.'

That was an interesting point, I thought as I downed

my last pint. Horror films confronted the ordinary with the strange and terrible. A film that made the ordinary appear strange and terrible wasn't horror. It was realism, of a kind that focused on the intrinsic misery of life. A dream was realistic in the same way. The film had been in black and white, like a dream. I'd had quite a few drinks by this time.

I walked back into the city centre with Ray and Karen, a film student from Walsall who'd seen *Last House on the Left* nine times at special cinema club screenings. I'd been to the electric screening; both the film and the hype surrounding it had made me think of Mark E. Smith's line about competitive plagiarism. But what do I know? All around us, the old shops of the jewellery quarter were shuttered, their visions hidden behind the screen.

Karen was swapping *The League of Gentlemen* quotes with Ray as we crossed over the canal bridge on Livery Street. Through the gaps in the stone wall, I could see moonlight reflected on the still water. But there was no moon. Confused, I stopped and leant over the canal. Dirty colours were stirring in the water: swirls of blue and green from spilt oil. The light seemed to come from below the surface. Suddenly an odour of decay and split stone touched my face. Bile trickled into my mouth, freezing me.

'Y'all right, Martin?' Ray was standing just behind me. He probably thought I'd drunk too much. He was probably right. I stared helplessly at the fading whorls of colour, the lost fingerprints. A name rose from the depths; I held onto it.

'Yeah, okay,' I said. We walked on slowly. 'Ray, do you know someone called W. Padgett? A journalist, used to write for *Screen Bizarre*?'

'God, there's a name from the past.' He frowned. 'Think I met him back in the late seventies. Will Padgett, yeah. I'm showing my age now. I was in college. This strange little guy with round glasses half an inch thick, really short-sighted, came to a screening of *The Tenant* and weirded us out in the pub afterwards with his theories about it.

'Back then, he used to write articles about obscure European directors. He was working on a huge book about what he called "the cinema of the unconscious", but something went wrong. I heard he was doing drugs. He started writing long paranoid letters to *Fortean Times*, attacking one of their writers: a guy called Ben Fitzworth who wrote features on black magic and weird cults. Then it came out that Fitzworth was really Padgett himself, writing under another name. He sort of faded out after that. God knows what he's doing now.'

'Do you know where he lives?' I asked, not sure why I wanted to know.

'He used to live somewhere on the Thames Estuary. Probably still there, unless he's been sectioned. I'm sure he's on the net, using another name. Not that I'm one to talk.'

'What was his theory about *The Tenant*?' Karen asked. By now we were walking up Snow Hill, past red-glowing restaurants and nightclubs that were slowly taking in queues of shivering teenagers. A black freight train rattled past on a bridge above the roadway.

'It was something about France,' Ray said. 'How Polanski felt when he came to France. 'Cause some of us thought *Repulsion* was a better film. Padgett said *Repulsion* was just a study of one person's madness, but *The Tenant* was about the persecution of outsiders. Polish guy Trelkovsky goes mad because everyone in the building is trying to *drive* him mad. He's a sacrifice. The building is doing it to him as well. It's the stored psychic energy of centuries of hatred, all focused on one victim after another.'

'Fuckin' hell,' Karen said. 'I thought it was just Polanski finding an excuse to dress up like a woman.'

Ray shrugged his rounded shoulders. 'Funny how you remember things,' he said. 'I can't remember what I did yesterday or what I'm supposed to do tomorrow. But I can remember stuff like that even though it's totally useless. Why?'

'Maybe your mind's telling you to change your life,' Karen said. She was lurching more dangerously with every step. We'd come to the beginning of Colmore Row, where cars rose staring from the shadows of the tunnel. Ray and Karen went on to the row of pale bus shelters on the other side. I walked through the green-painted façade of Snow Hill Station, down the glass-lined corridor to the dark steps that led down to the platform. Where I had plenty of time to sober up, as the last train was half an hour late.

I've lost count of the number of things in my life – dates, films, meals, work appointments – I've missed because of delayed or cancelled trains. If I'd been an alcoholic or a junkie, I don't think I could have bigger holes in my diary. Being a passenger teaches you that life is random and nothing can be counted on. These were the bitter thoughts I always warmed myself with at such times, sitting in the waiting-room and trying to ignore the one-sided conversations going on around me. I'm not sure which disturbed me more: the people with tiny phones clamped to their cheekbones like growths, or the people who seemed to be talking to thin air.

When I finally reached Tyseley Station, the four platforms were deserted. I climbed the steps and paused as something gave way under my foot. Suddenly I could smell rotting wood and stone, an overwhelming reek that almost made me throw up. I didn't associate it with the station; it reminded me of the pavilion at my secondary school, the lukewarm showers and the pale, mud-streaked adolescent flesh. Boys like unfinished sculptures in wet clay, their cocks shrivelled by the cold.

I have one more memory of that night. It seems more important now than it did at the time. I woke up before dawn; my mouth was dry, and I needed to piss. The bathroom was downstairs, at the back of the house. When I switched on the light, my first impression was of a shadow coming apart on the vinyl floor. There was a mass of woodlice there, two or three dozen, unusually small and dark. They got in through the skirting-board, but not usually in such numbers. I seized a broom and swiped at them, as if they were a dream that action could dissolve. Some of them crept frantically in all directions, their long feelers twitching and probing the cold air. Others lay still, their legs drawn under their shells, perhaps already dead. They made me feel the house was not a place for people to live in. If I shared the dark and chill of their territory, I couldn't really be human.

The Electric Cinema was in a backstreet close to New Street Station. It had formerly been the Jacey, which screened cartoons on Sunday mornings and soft porn at all other times. That had been closed for years when Aston University destroyed the Triangle Cinema, and a few refugees paddled their tiny celluloid boats into the city centre and started the Electric. It had a brick-red façade; above the jagged lettering of its name was a balcony where naked wax dummies were frozen in postures of dancing, embracing and fighting. Inside, the shabby décor and shaky projection betrayed a serious lack of funds. But it offered real coffee and home-made cakes, and the most adventurous film programme anywhere in Birmingham.

The evening I went to talk to Barry, he was sorting through books and magazines for the coffee shop. A tall man, he walked with a perpetual stoop that owed something to a lifetime of cinema seats. His glasses were broken and had been mended with Scotch tape. Two films were in progress, so there was noone much in the foyer. I bought a cup of bitter coffee and some desiccated chocolate cake. 'Do you read a lot of film magazines?' I asked him.

He squinted at me, as if my face was lacking something. 'When I can. It's useful for films I can't get to see. Foreign stuff especially.'

'Have you ever seen any of Jean Rien's films?' Barry frowned at me. 'I've seen one,' I said. '*L'éclipse des sens*. On a pirate video. Read an article about him. But nobody I know seems to know any of his films. It's almost like he never existed.'

'That's because he didn't,' Barry said. 'It's a hoax.' there was a note of anger in his voice. 'There's this kind of cult. People who pretend they've seen his films, write articles about them. They usually claim he invoked some... sort of god that's trying to cover its tracks. I don't know why people feel the need to make up this stuff.'

19

'But I saw the film. There were these four youngsters living in an old house. And some creature that was watching them. Like a throwback, or a mutant. They were going mad. I didn't understand it, but it scared me.'

'Sounds like a few kids who'd smoked too much dope. They'll have shot it themselves, probably using some of the articles about "Jean Rien" to guide them. Fakes always generate more fakes to make the first fakes seem real. Like that Roswell shit a few years ago. But what I don't understand is why these films sound so dark. Hoaxes are usually upbeat, that's how they trap so many idiots. Ask yourself this: if those films were real, why would they be remembered? Do we really need a cinema of total despair? Films can help us make sense of life. These… non-existent films don't make sense, full stop. Who needs them?'

'Will Padgett does, apparently.'

'Well, he's completely mad. If that's even his real name. People like that are best avoided.' Barry shrugged uneasily and returned to his careful sorting and tidying of the contents of the tiny shop. I watched him for a minute, then walked out to the bus stop. The roadway was streaked with frost.

———

The demonstration – or vigil, as the organisers called it – at Tyseley Station took place late on a Saturday night. There were about thirty of us, wearing fluorescent radiation warning stickers on our coats, handing out leaflets about the nuclear train to drunken, bemused passengers as they emerged from the station. It was a quiet night.

As the wind sharpened its nails, we huddled together in the shelter of the Victorian frontage. The light from the streetlamp matched the yellow of the warning stickers. Judith made a cave of her hands and blew into it. She was shivering. This was as close as I ever got to feeling part of a community. I had a strange impression that our movements were being controlled by someone or something beneath our feet, down on the platform.

When a freight train approached, some of us went down the wooden steps to have a look at it. The train carrying radioactive waste wasn't due for three hours, but you couldn't rely on the timetables. Nobody was waiting on the platform. The train was unmarked, a seemingly endless chain of iron-bound carriages tearing past at a frantic rate. Its icy slipstream pulled at my face, and I turned away. Judith was behind me, a silhouette against the distant station light.

The train went on and on, its wheels grinding out a lullaby in thrash metal. None of us moved. Our own shadows masked our faces. I could smell decay again, so powerful I thought the light was rotting. There should have been a presence down here, a guiding spirit. But there was nothing.

FOUR

In those days I was working as a sub-editor for the *Warwick View*, a weekly free newspaper that relied on advertising for its income. I couldn't afford to live in Warwick, and wouldn't really have wanted to. It's an old town that has gradually been converted by wealthy commuters into a model village, packed with antique shops and expensive restaurants. I quite enjoyed the cosy insularity of the *View*: it was a refuge from bad and twisted news. But sometimes they carried echoes of the outside world. For example, one story reported that a woman had been mugged by a 'bogus asylum seeker' in Leamington. How did they know so much about a man who hadn't been arrested or identified? Did he wear a sweatshirt that said *I FOOLED THE HOME OFFICE*? Were there torture scars on his arms that washed off in the rain?

Like practically every other newspaper, the *View* declared the famous 'smoking gun' video to be 'absolute proof' that the bombing of Afghanistan was justified and necessary. If you've not seen this particular item of evidence, it's a camcorder home movie of Bin Laden sitting in a cave, laughing and bragging about how the World Trade Center was destroyed. At one point he uses his hands to parody the way the towers collapsed. And this video was apparently left lying around in a Kabul house for American soldiers to find. I'm surprised they didn't find it in Turin.

Of course, Bin Laden almost certainly *had* masterminded the attacks on New York and the Pentagon. But that was no longer the point. The Americans needed a totem, an icon, that would silence all questions about their devastation of a virtually unarmed country. Six thousand dead civilians, whole towns and villages wiped off the map. This cheap fragment of computer manipulated footage, with its blurred images and barely audible soundtrack, was the answer. And reality itself had become thin and transparent, like a strip of celluloid.

Around that time, there was a major anti-war march in London. Judith and I went down on the coach that left from Sparkbrook. A lot of the passengers were Moslems, their mood a combination of anger and unease. It was a long, tiring march and there wasn't a lot to feel confident about. The sight of Trafalgar Square filled with people was briefly overwhelming; I felt inspired by that tidal sense of purpose that comes from being a part of something much bigger. But as soon as I stopped moving, the stone landscape made me think of decay. The smell of ashes from a burning flag choked me.

Judith still didn't seem comfortable staying at my house, but I got the feeling she was afraid of being alone.

She suffered from seasonal depression, though it was more bad weather – grey skies, continual rain – than cold that brought her down. Unlike me, she loved working: her screen was a world she could influence, changing light and shade to bring a page to life. Away from that, the environment weighed her down. To lift her mood, I bought a Tiffany lamp, a new magenta sofa and some cushion covers for the living room I still hoped would become ours. One of the worrying differences between us was that I knew my way around the blues, but Judith didn't. I could fall into the safety-net of vodka and Leonard Cohen albums, safe in the reassurance of a monochrome world. When Judith was down, she got lost. She'd panic, convinced there was no way back to the light.

In February, I managed to contact Will Padgett. It was Ray's remark about *Fortean Times* that put me on his track. Their website contained a link to an obscure, jerry-built site for film obsessives called *Nameless Frames*. This site contained a number of murky stills from Jean Rien films that crashed my computer whenever I tried to view their captions. One still showed a girl with dark glasses being chased through a crumbling brick alley by a mob of pale, stumbling men with blank expressions. I felt sure I recognised it.

Most of the site's text files were corrupt or trapped behind photos, but there was an isolated paragraph at the bottom of one page that I could make out. Under a blurred silhouette of a deformed or agonised figure, the text read:

> The cinema of Jean Rien is a window into a world of
> instinct, an *Umwelt*. To see that world clearly, we must
> let go of what makes us audience members or critics.
> We become witnesses, and have to pass through the
> dark in order to survive. The shadows of Rien's films are
> a passageway to the realm that has always existed inside
> us.
> – Ben Fitzworth

When I clicked on the by-line, it turned out to be a link
to a cheaply made, black-and-white e-zine called *Frameless
Names*. Its pages flickered too badly to be legible, but
appeared to contain a mixture of anarchist gonzo journalism
and surreal photography. The list of contributors on the
final page included Stewart Home, Hertzan Chimera and
W. Padgett. Once again, the name was a hyperlink: it led
to *padgett@neregretterien.fsnet.co.uk*. Looking back, I can't
remember my thoughts when I clicked on the dim red letters
of that name. If I had known how much I would lose, would
I still have made the contact? I don't know.

A fortnight later, I caught an evening train to Gravesend by
way of London. There was frost on the ground; parts of the
Thames Estuary were frozen. The lights of buildings wavered
in the misty dark. The streets between the station and the pub
were slippery and barely lit; I felt like I was walking underwater.
There was no colour anywhere in the picture, and the air tasted
of salt. Suddenly I thought of the dreadful week Judith and
I had spent in Devon the year before. The long anonymous
poem, *Views of a Black Earth*, that a previous occupant of the
house had left for us to find. Books can't change your life, but
they can ruin your holiday. Perhaps I still hadn't shaken off the

depression of that time. Yet I hadn't thought about it in months. It must have been the Thames Estuary that was reminding me of the Devon coastline, its grey water and polluted breath.

The pub that Will Padgett had suggested as a rendezvous was called The Black Dog. It was one of those mood-saturated urban pubs that hadn't yet been decked out in bogus signifiers of history. With its pitted mahogany panelling and black staircase railings, it vaguely resembled a mid-century railway station. Large storage heaters kept the air uncomfortably warm. A tape of sixties classics was playing from a concealed speaker: Dusty Springfield, The Animals, Procol Harum.

I was halfway through a pint of London Pride when a balding man in his forties walked past me to the bar. Having secured a pint, he turned and peered nervously at the shadows of the lounge. His thick, round glasses accentuated the roundness of his face, and his skin had a boyish glow accentuated by the greying stubble on his jawline and throat. I noticed that he was clutching a beat-up copy of *Fangoria*. He walked past me and fiddled with the cigarette machine. I realised he was too nervous to say hello.

When he turned round, with no cigarettes, I stood up. 'Will Padgett?'

'That's as good a name as any. You're Martin Swann, I take it?'

'I am. But I'd rather just talk.' He blinked at me in confusion. 'Good to meet you,' I said. 'If it really is you.'

'I think it is.' He put his pint and magazine down carefully on the black table. 'These days it's hard to be sure.'

I suppressed the impulse to find a Celtic double entendre in that. What was wrong with me? Padgett sat down and knocked back a respectable fraction of his pint. 'Anything good in that magazine?' I asked.

'Feature on *Dagon*, the new Stuart Gordon film. Shot on location, in a perpetual rainstorm. They've placed Innsmouth on the Spanish coast.'

'I didn't know you were a horror enthusiast.'

Behind the lenses, his eyes were vague and shadowy. 'I'm not,' he said. 'Or not when they call it that. What's the point of telling people to expect horror? Takes all the mystery out of it. You might as well just live your own life. That ends in death and pain as well, but we manage not to face it.'

'Is that why a director like Rien appeals to you so much? Because the horrors are embedded in real life?'

Padgett glanced to one side, as if afraid we were being watched. Then he laughed uneasily. 'If you knew more about Rien, you wouldn't say that,' he said. 'In fact, you wouldn't talk about him at all. Which of his films have you seen?'

I thought about it. 'That one – oh, you know. There's a piano. Haven't I told you?' I'm never good with titles.'

Padgett stared at me for a few seconds. Then he finished his pint. 'There have been interviews with Rien,' he said. 'Features on his work. But you won't find any of them in print. If you trace a reference to a particular magazine, you'll find back copies of it are unavailable or the relevant pages are missing. Objectively speaking, his films don't exist.

'Occasionally, groups get together who know his work. But as soon as they take on a formal identity as Rien societies, and especially when they start to publish anything, they disappear. Their members just forget that the films ever existed. Like a dream they've woken up from.

'I have an A4 poster from the Exeter University Film Society in 1979, advertising a screening of Rien's film *La nuit qui brille*. I was the only person who went to see it. None of the film society came. The projectionist was an hour late, and he'd brought a copy of *Eraserhead*. Suddenly, a dozen people turned up expecting to see that. I kept the poster as evidence, but didn't show it to the projectionist. Even then, I was afraid of them getting onto me.'

Abruptly, he stood up. 'Another pint?'

'Er... yes please.' I could stay until closing time, since the last train back to Birmingham left at midnight. At last, the hidden world of Rien was opening up to me. Though I wasn't sure why it mattered, or why I needed a guide. Somehow the rules had changed.

When Padgett returned with two narrow pint glasses, I asked him, 'So did you ever get to see that film they didn't show in Exeter?'

He nodded. '*La nuit qui brille*. The night that shines. Yes, I finally got to see it in Amsterdam ten years later. It's a short film, barely an hour, about an infectious disease that causes blindness in a small town. As their vision corrodes, the people begin to glimpse some kind of angel in the air above them. There may be a single creature or a whole community. Like a child made of faintly discoloured light, its arms crossed.

'By the end of the film, everyone is completely blind and there are no angels. Only rats and black hailstones and mould creeping up the walls. And the dark sea beating on the doors of the houses. I heard a rumour that Rien shot it on the coast of Scotland, because no French town was bleak enough.'

'How come you can remember all that?' I asked.

He shrugged. 'Maybe I'm not really a person. I don't mean I'm something else. I just don't belong to the day or to the night. I'm always stuck in the doorway. Watching the traffic go back and forth.'

That made more sense to me than I could really account for. I got the next round in while trying to frame another question. When I returned, Padgett had gone to the gents'. I flicked through his copy of *Fangoria*, looking at prosthetic masks and smoky, filtered light. When he came back, I asked him, 'Who is suppressing Rien's films?'

'That's a paranoid question,' he said austerely. 'Do you think people are suppressing the films? Have you met these unseen censors? Hung with seraphim whose mothballs crinkled in the rusted score?' His hand trembled as he lifted the pint to his mouth.

'But you said there was a *they*,' I said, feeling oddly childish.

Padgett shook his head and gazed at me patiently. 'Not the censors. The fans. Listen, whoever you think you are. I used to think people were dedicated to obliterating every trace of Rien's films. Then I met a man called Ben Fitzworth, who knew more than me about Rien. Far more. He believes that all of Rien's films are hints of an entity. A power, a god perhaps. Something mysterious and terrible, glimpsed only in distorted shadows. Negatives. Views of a black earth. And whatever it is, it doesn't want to be seen.

'For years, I went along with Fitzworth. But he's a fuck-up. A heroin addict, a pathological liar. He stole my wallet and slept with my wife. I'll never believe a word he says again.' Padgett shut his eyes, drained his pint in a long painful swallow.

'So what do you believe now?'

'In a moment.' The bell rang thinly for last orders. 'Another pint? Or maybe a short?'

'Double scotch. Thanks.' The alcohol gave me a sense of being about to pierce the veil. Maybe this time, for once, it wasn't only the alcohol. I could see fragments of dark life stirring in the cracked wall and skirting-board by the storage heater. Unnerved, I put my feet on the lower rung of the stool.

Padgett came back with two glasses full of amber light. We drank in silence. The jukebox had shifted from sixties pop to the trembling wail of ska and bluebeat. I waited for his revelation; but he only gestured towards the bar, where the somnolent barman was still pouring drinks.

I staggered to the bar on legs that felt like unjointed stilts, and bought two glasses of vodka whose clarity guided me back to the table. He watched my drunken movements with amused tolerance, then lifted his glass, emptied it in one considered gulp, and said, 'Martin, all I can say is this. When Orpheus turned to see his beloved emerging from the underworld, he was only protecting himself. But later, at the awards ceremony, he pretended it had all been a mistake. Everything we search for, every holy grail, is something we cannot afford to find.' He lifted his empty glass to the light.

The pub was slowly clearing. The barman took the glasses from our table and wished us goodnight. Outside, the streets were glowing with rain. Sodium lamps burned holes in the mist. Padgett still didn't appear drunk. He shook my hand politely and said, 'Goodnight. I hope you catch your train.'

I didn't want to say goodnight. I wanted to go with him, wherever he would lead me. 'Where do I go now?' I asked.

'The station's down that way, by the park.' He pointed to an avenue where the trees shook rain from their dark heads.

'I mean with the films. With Rien. Do I just forget it all?'

Padgett gazed at me for a moment, his eyes blurred with reflected light. 'Maybe,' he said. 'There are worse things than forgetting.' He seemed about to walk away; but then, as a car drove past us, he shouted over its voiceless roar; 'There's one Rien film I don't think has ever been screened. It's called *La mort des témoins*. His last film. I don't know where he made it. But the only way to see it is to go there.'

He turned and began to walk back to the main road. I shouted after him, 'What does the title mean?'

His glasses flashed in the half-light. 'The death of the witnesses.' Then he was gone. It was nearly midnight, and I was too drunk to find the station. But within a minute, I hailed a black cab and sat curled up in the darkness of its back seat, trying not to vomit.

I didn't know why I was so drawn to Padgett. Men didn't attract me – and certainly not middle-aged men who looked like monks. But there was something about the way he'd blurred or disguised his identity that made him different, that gave him power. Was he the guide that Ian Curtis had waited for?

Now, of course, I can see that it wasn't Padgett at all that I was attracted to. He was just a face in the twilight. I could see the night beyond him. I might have understood it even then, if I hadn't been quite so shitfaced.

I spent the next half-hour on the platform, walking slowly back and forth in the drizzling rain to stop myself throwing up. The only other person there was a station attendant who was picking up rubbish with a pair of metal pincers attached to a stick. Eventually a train arrived, but it went straight through without stopping. The vibration shook the windows of the unlit waiting room. I went back to the ticket office to ask what was happening; but the attendant had vanished.

Around one o'clock, a young couple walked sleepily onto the platform. After trying the waiting room and the toilets – both were locked – they sheltered in one of the doorways and began to fuck. I sat at the other end of the platform, watching the empty line; but I could still hear them. As I sobered up, the station lost its comforting glow and reverted to a dull, metallic grey. The walls were spotted with black mould. The rain smelt of petrol and decay.

I wondered what Judith was doing now. Was she drunk, listening to the stereo, watching reality TV? I thought of her curled up on the sofa cushions, asleep. Then, for no reason, I saw rain dripping through her ceiling, falling like insects to darken her pillow. I opened my eyes and stared into the lightless tunnel at the end of the platform. I could hear the metallic pulse of a distant train, growing louder; but I couldn't see its lights.

When the grey windowless carriages with their yellow warning signs rattled out of the tunnel, drawing to a halt at the red signal light, I turned away in disgust. *There are no more passenger trains, only freight trains. Waste coats our world like a sleeve.* Then a word flickered across the window of the unlit waiting-room. I couldn't read it, but it made me think of the Tyseley Station and its sealed Victorian waiting rooms. Confused, I looked back at the freight train.

Every third carriage had a placard marked 'BIRMINGHAM'. What did Birmingham need more waste for – didn't it have enough of its own? Maybe it was a consignment of essential materials. Shattered bricks. Dog food. Wood-chip wallpaper. St George flags. Doves made of vacuum-formed plastic. By now, I was sober enough to know what a night spent on a Gravesend platform would be like. And drunk enough for the alternative to seem feasible.

The carriages were open at the top. I couldn't see what they contained. I ran across the platform, jumped up and caught the rim of the carriage with my hands. My trailing feet kicked the metal side; it reverberated like a steel drum. I drew my legs into a crouch, then tipped myself forward. The steel floor was covered by some kind of sacking; I landed on my right shoulder, and the pain dazed me for a minute or so. As the freight train jerked into motion, I closed my eyes and curled up in the recovery position. The sound of my breathing seemed to echo from the metallic walls.

A half-moon was visible through a moist scar of cloud. I could just make out a number of elongated objects leaning against the carriage walls, like carpets or wooden logs. Had I somehow managed not to fall against any of them, or was that how I'd hurt myself? Something made me reluctant to touch them. But if I stayed on the floor, they might fall on me. So I struggled to my feet, just as the train reached a built-up area where the moonlight was outshone by sodium light. It caught the standing objects, painted their bony faces yellow.

As far as I could tell, they were awake. That was how they stayed upright. But they hardly seemed aware of me. The light didn't catch their eyes, but I could see their gaunt chests stirring faintly as they breathed. I stood in the middle of the carriage, trying not to move. I hoped the train wouldn't jerk to a halt and throw me against one of them. As long as they gave no sign of having seen me, I could pretend I hadn't seen them.

An hour or so later, the train stopped. I climbed out of the carriage and, more by luck than with the help of my frozen muscles, fell onto the platform. It was Milton Keynes Central. I spent the rest of the night walking the featureless streets, passing office blocks and traffic islands, seeing no one except the teenage prostitutes and their minders who hung around the train station until dawn. Whenever I stopped walking, I began to shake. The pale streaks of cloud couldn't cover up the moon's decay.

I heard from Will Padgett twice more. A fortnight after our meeting in Gravesend, he sent me an e-mail with the title *The witnesses are gone.* Under a crude, badly scanned image of a human eye, he wrote:

> Hi Martin. I wish you good luck in your quest for Rien. But always remember this: the auteur theory is the death of the witness. If the scene has an author, then those who witness it are merely an audience. Do you remember reading Lovecraft or Machen for the first time and believing, just for a moment, that what you were reading was not fiction? That some documents of another reality had fallen into your hands? That these stories not only changed their genre, they changed everything? And now the same stories appear in corrected editions, with long

introductions and scholarly footnotes by S.T. Joshi, the
suspension of disbelief is impossible. Ask yourself how
it would be if Rien's films were part of a canon, on a par
with Tarkovsky or Franju. A season at the National Film
Theatre. Late-night screenings on Channel 4, with Mark
Cousins trying to shape the meaning of each film with his
hands. It would be nice. But something essential would
have been lost.

A month later, when I came back from Paris, there was a
final message from Padgett in my inbox. It said simply: *Rien
and his films never existed. There is nothing to investigate. Forget
it.* By then, I was able to understand what he meant by that.

FIVE

In late summer, we had another of those heatwaves that sweep away all our assumptions about the British climate. Perhaps they're a vision of the near future. The heat kept me awake at night and made me sleepy all day, my head filled with shadow. I had to put ant powder on the kitchen floor. When Judith and I slept together, the bed felt as sticky and uncomfortable as a polluted beach. Though she never mentioned it, I knew she was thinking of our weekend in Dorset the year before.

We'd rented a house in a mostly wooded area near the coast. On paper, it looked wonderful: the perfect antidote to expressways and sodium lighting. But the reality was a kind of self-catering abscess. It rained most of the time. The air was lukewarm and brackish, as if it had a mild fever. The house clearly hadn't been cleaned in years; every surface was coated with a film of dust held in place by moisture. The windows were smeared, darkening the outside world. There was a streak of black mould across the bedroom ceiling.

When the rain eased off, we walked in the forest or caught a bus to the coast. Judith took black-and-white photographs of trees glittering with rain, beaches spotted with dead jellyfish. She sold a few of them later. Away from the city, we felt slightly inhibited by the stillness of nature: it was difficult to talk outdoors. We walked along sandy beaches or cliff paths, ignoring the pollution, until our legs ached with fatigue. We held hands, like children, as we entered the twilight of the restless woods.

In the past, I'd found holidays gave me a chance to get away from myself and become more open to the atmosphere and culture of a strange place. But this time the environment took away my confidence. I no longer knew how to react or feel. Without the familiar world to remind me, I didn't even seem to know who I was. The place had the same effect on Judith. She talked a little about her ex-husband: 'It started with him trying to undermine my friends, make me feel they weren't a good influence on me. By the end, he was getting up early to intercept my mail. I complained to the postman that my letters had been torn open. Then I realised it was him.'

When rain or nightfall trapped us in the house, we seemed unable to leave each other alone. We fucked every night and morning, despite the heat and the creased, piled cotton sheets. It relieved the tension that the decaying house created in us. In the evenings we cooked pasta and drank a lot: wine, brandy, gin. I remember Judith suggesting one night that the 'VSOP' on a bottle of French brandy was an apology, and both of us laughing for ages because we were wrecked. Drunk or not, the creaking of the house kept us awake at night. We talked about the family who might have lived there, and whose persistent footsteps we could hear. An old woman, a young couple, two children.

We might have been all right if it hadn't been for the book. The first night we were there, I found it in an old desk in the hallway. It was a thin volume with card wrappers, probably a limited edition, called *Views of a Black Earth*. No author name, publisher or date. Most of the two dozen pages were taken up by a long, dreamlike narrative poem. The rest were stark woodcuts: a willow tree, a rainstorm, a drowning woman. Judith and I both read it several times, but were unable to make much sense of it. So we started using it to interpret the landscape around us, as if it were a key to the claustrophobic romance we had trapped ourselves in. You do things like that when you're away from home and disorientated by alcohol and love.

I'm not sure I ever understood what *Views of a Black Earth* was about. It was like Eliot with travel sickness. The poem traced the four seasons through different places, using different voices. It began with an uneasy love affair:

We laughed, because we couldn't see the
tower in the mist.

As the heat crept in, love became sex and the sea became blood.

I wake; the grass
is rotten, soil is wet; the trees
are bare with night.

The rest of the poem described a world soaked through with decay. Rain falling in the night, washing the headstones blank.

The bonfire
smoke picks through the leaves, an old widow
looking for sons.

The dead leaves piling up until the trees sank and the fires went out. The ending was stark and enigmatic:

The guide has lost
his charges in the drifts. A candle
burns with many flames; and we
were drenched in winter rains last year.

We discussed who could have written the poem. It seemed full of experience at one level, but naïve at another. Judith said the author had either read too much or lived too much, but not both. I felt he or she had been quite disturbed – perhaps the book hadn't just been a poem to its author. We quoted bits of it to each other while walking in the decaying forest. In the house, the poem got into our heads and made us feel threatened. The close air and the rainstorms frightened us, because they made the images of views of a black earth seem real. When we left the house, I wanted to bury the thin book in the mould of the forest floor. But we had to pack up in a hurry after oversleeping, so I just left it in the desk.

Since coming back to Birmingham, we hadn't talked much about the holiday. It was like an illness that we'd shared, bringing us closer together but providing no images for the photograph album. And neither of us had mentioned the book at all. But now, I was beginning to see how it was linked to the decaying world I'd been living in since I discovered the videotape in my shed. Lying beside Judith one night, unable to sleep, I became certain that the author of *Views of a Black Earth* was Will Padgett. Who else could it be?

But I didn't tell Judith that. I didn't want her to think I was obsessed with Padgett and become jealous. And maybe he hadn't really used the title of the poem in our conversation. I'd been very drunk. There could be more than one mad person in the world. What I did tell Judith, over breakfast the next morning, was that our week in the Devon forest had been rather like a Jean Rien film. 'In the film I saw, a piano was used to play some kind of weird atonal music. It wasn't a normal piano. And there was a book written in runes. From what I've found out, Rien's films always have mysterious objects that hold secrets. And strange creatures that come from somewhere else. Like the black jellyfish we found on the beach in Dorset. And that book. *Views of a Black Earth*.'

Judith looked up from her bowl of Alpen muesli. 'What book? We didn't take any books to Dorset.'

'The book we found there. The poem. All those weird lines we quoted to each other. About death and decay.'

Judith frowned. 'Called *Views of a Black Earth*? Sounds like a Public Enemy album. You never showed it to me. I wouldn't have touched any book from that house anyway. They were probably all infested with weevils or silverfish or something. Vile place.' She was quiet the rest of that morning; perhaps the memory depressed her.

The news was depressing us too. As the first anniversary of the attack on New York approached, the US government

41

was talking about invading Iraq. Their stated reason was that Iraq was refusing to surrender its 'weapons of mass destruction'. The more the arms inspectors failed to track down these weapons, the more evidence that provided of a deadly concealment. Had Spike Milligan still been alive, he could have sued the White House for plagiarism. *That's because they're* hiding, *Min*. A false reality was beating at us from the outside and corroding us from within. What was left of us – me, Judith, Padgett, everyone – was no thicker than a cinema screen.

SIX

For some months now, I'd been collecting minor film magazines and festival programmes from France, Spain and Italy in the hope of tracking down one of Rien's films. In early September, I received an envelope containing the last two issues of *Cahier du cinéma*, a programme for a science fiction film convention in Poitiers, and several battered-looking flyers for individual cinemas or screenings. One of the flyers was so poorly printed I could hardly read it. Beside a stark silhouette of a narrow house was the title *La maison noire* and an address in the Marais district of Paris. A series of autumn dates and film titles followed; none of the films, or even the directors, was familiar to me. At the bottom of the first column, I could just make out:

```
Septembre 29: trois films de Jean Rien (11:00 du soir)
La nuit qui brille + Abhorré de la lune + Son drapeau noir
```

I'd never been to Paris. The finances didn't look encouraging, but then it occurred to me that I didn't need to book a hotel room. The three films would probably take me through most of the night, and I could get by on coffee until the first available flight back. That would save me paperwork as well as money. I'd often missed a night's sleep in my student days, because of an essay deadline or just sheer excitement. Or passion, a few times. You paid for it in the end. I booked a return flight at the travel agent's in Acocks Green, to reach Charles de Gaulle airport at four p.m. I'd have to come back the next afternoon.

Judith thought it was a great idea. 'If a night of three films doesn't help you get that crap out of your system, nothing will.' I asked her if she'd like to come with me, make a weekend of it, and she looked at me as if I'd suggested having sex in a glass tank. 'Why? I don't want to see those films.' I thought she was missing the point, but later I realised she was being more honest than I could be about my own state of mind. It was like the time we'd tried to make love and failed, and she'd said, 'How can you be inside me when you're not even inside yourself?'

The security at Birmingham airport was pretty intense, and they took my camera apart without explanation. The plane left an hour late. It rose through an inverted forest of rain into the grey earth of the clouds, then emerged from a sunlit plateau of ice. I had no idea what was beneath us: land, water or outer space. The airline staff gave us plastic boxes containing ham rolls and fruit. It was oddly dreamlike to be surrounded by cold and not feel it. If the plane crashed, would the dream go on forever?

The sense of unreality was heightened by the change in time zone, which made the hour's flight time disappear. The train from Charles de Gaulle airport to Paris passed through a flattened landscape of factories and fields. It was still daylight when the view was enclosed, broken up and multiplied by the city's tall grey buildings. Clutching my little travelling-bag nervously, I made my way through the crowded streets. The dark façade of each tenement building was divided into sections by iron railings, like a strip of frames.

I wondered how many times Jean Rien had wandered these streets. What I knew of his films suggested that he'd lived and worked mostly in small towns. But as a filmmaker, he must have come here to meet people, arrange things. This was where his career had taken shape. The dense, rather studious architecture of this restless city might hold some key to Rien's mind. Gripped by a kind of paranoid energy, I walked through the Marais district as sodium light replaced daylight. I saw old churches jewelled with lamps, porn cinemas with doorways that were neon vaginas, bars crowded with students listening to live music, bookshops with leather-bound volumes packed like cobblestones behind dusty glass. A girl in a tight red sweater beckoned me to follow her into an alley; I walked on, mindful of my slim wallet and limited grasp of the international language of trouble. But not of Judith, which worried me.

In a small café that was also a bookshop, I found a paperback anthology of horror stories – American, in translation. 'La cité sous le mer' by H.P. Lovecraft turned out to be 'Dagon', as a glance at the last line confirmed. I stumbled through the tale while drinking bottled beer and eating a plate of shellfish. I found Lovecraft's aversion to seafood as hard to understand as his fascist sympathies, though somewhat easier to condone. According to the pocket guidebook I'd brought with me, Hitler had planned to destroy Paris; but in the end he'd decided it was unnecessary. I tried to imagine these streets blown apart, people crawling through an abyss of broken stone and fire. I must have forgotten to pack my lighten up pills.

The beer had sharpened my appetite for alcohol. As I made my way uncertainly towards the street of *La maison noire* – and map-reading had never been one of my skills – each darkened bar seemed to call out to me. The streetlights were too bright; I felt exposed. In all I stopped four times on my way to the cinema, and the only bar I remember with any clarity was on the corner of a blind alley. The interior was shadowy and crowded with men – a few talking, but most just standing. There were no seats. Some kind of austere techno pulsed through the smoky air. It was evidently a gay bar for Protestants. Wooden stairs led up to an unlit second floor; as I watched, a man descended with an air of inviolable calm. I drained my glass and climbed the stairs.

A doorway was half-concealed by hanging strips of some black fabric. I stepped through into a dimly lit room full of silent men. Some were making love in pairs; others were watching, or waiting for an opportunity. The air was a garden of scents: cologne, sweat, aftershave, cigarettes, hairspray and cum. I watched for a while, but couldn't move. It reminded me of the hidden passengers on the freight train. The nameless, the lost. Though no doubt they were dead nice when you got to know them.

The cinema was a narrow two-storey building with its windows blacked out, as if in preparation for an air-raid. A number of tiny glass-framed posters were displayed around the door, including one for Rien's *Abhorré de la lune*: a view through the bars of a cell in a high building, looking down over a small town. The buildings were corroded, too thin, about to collapse. There were several black towers, each with a few barred windows. The stars overhead were rippled, as if seen through water. The poster was a faded image behind a speckled sheet of glass. None of the posters seemed current. I would have assumed the cinema to be derelict if it hadn't been open.

Inside, there were no posters or listings: just black walls and a flickering red mercury light. A middle-aged woman was sitting behind a glass screen, reading an art magazine of some kind. 'Les trois films de Jean Rien?' I asked. She nodded, as if my request had confirmed her suspicions about me, then asked me for ten francs. Then she leant forward and pointed to the staircase behind me. It led to a pair of wooden swing doors, behind which was a small auditorium with a dozen or so rows of seats. I could see a few people sitting in the half- light. Nobody tore up my ticket.

The seats were impregnated with smoke, and not only from tobacco. The air-conditioning was either broken or non-existent. I took my jacket off and loosened the top button of my shirt. Without warning, the screen turned from black to sepia and a film began. Presumably a trailer. A teenage girl, dressed only in a pale slip, was crawling through some kind of narrow underground passage. Tree-roots and bones poked up through shattered tiles. It seemed to be an old black-and-

47

white film, the print marred by flecks and cracks – unless it was some kind of pastiche, like Guy Maddin's *Tales From the Gimli Hospital*. Perhaps it was the first of the three Rien films; it would be just like him to open with a dream sequence.

Around me, more people were moving stealthily from the aisles to the seats; their figures were bent over, as if they were part of the film. Now the girl had reached some kind of chamber in which she could stand up, but the way forward was blocked by an iron gate. As she stared through the bars, two thuggish men in black masks approached from behind her. They tied her pale hands to the bars, tore off her slip and took her brutally, one after the other. Her face remained still, untinged by either distress or pleasure.

The air in the increasingly crowded auditorium was so close, you could have sliced it to fill sandwiches. I began to fan myself with a newspaper. The pages made a clicking sound; a man sitting behind me sighed knowingly. As the second of the two attackers reached his climax, the scene dissolved. The same girl was lying in a single bed, part of a girls' dormitory. Her eyes opened, and she raised herself to gaze longingly though the barred window. The picture was in colour now, with the travel-sick realism of a video camera. Behind the girl's back, some other girls were giggling. Small hands reached from behind to caress her; she was pulled back onto the bed. A dressing-gown cord was used to tie her hands to the iron bedstead.

My reluctant, but undeniable, attention was distracted by a young woman moving past me on her hands and knees. I began to stand up, but she pushed my thighs back onto the seat. Then she pointed to her mouth and whispered, 'Cent francs.' Her dark hair made her face look impossibly thin in the half-light. I shook my head, and she moved on. The contact brought me back to myself, and I felt cheated – though of what, I wasn't sure. Trying not to look at the screen, I rose to my feet and stumbled towards the dark exit. What I'd seen couldn't be part of a Rien film. It was too real, too crude. It was hardcore.

I meant to complain, ask for a refund, maybe even say that I'd come from England to see the missing films. The woman behind the glass screen looked up as I approached, and I meant to say, 'Ca n'est pas Rien.' But my confusion and embarrassment made me say, 'Ca ne fait rien.' The woman shrugged and returned to her magazine. Feeling crushed, I left the cinema.

By now it was raining, which brought the city's lights closer but made the streets harder to distinguish. I began to retrace my steps, with no idea of where to go or how I'd get through the night. Under a streetlamp I paused to unfold the map, but raindrops blotted out the words within seconds. Then I became aware that someone was watching me. A tall, thin man around my own age, wearing a red leather jacket. He looked vaguely Mediterranean, or perhaps Arab. I realised he'd followed me out of the cinema.

'The film disappointed you,' he said. His intonation was slightly wooden, but his vowel sounds were more standard English than mine. 'It wasn't what you expected.'

'I bought a ticket to see three films by Jean Rien. You too?'

The stranger shook his head. 'The ticket seller is completely deaf. But no, they're not showing those films. In *La maison noire* they only show… fuck films. Someone has lied to you.' He smiled. 'It must have been because you were breathing.'

'Where can I get to see Rien's films?' I asked. 'Are there copies anywhere? Videos, maybe? Have you seen...?'

'I can help you find them,' he said. 'Come with me.' He walked on, quickly but cautiously, avoiding the drunks who were prowling in groups outside the bars. I had no choice but to follow him. He led me into an older part of the city, with grey churches and cobbled streets and flights of stone steps. I half expected to hear unearthly violin music coming from a tenement window. It's odd how much our perception of cities owes to stories and films. We talk about 'Dickensian' London as if it had some real existence beyond the page. Deep down, despite the evidence of our lives, we can't really believe that anything is ever made up.

At last, he stopped outside a narrow terraced house with the door and windows painted black. He rang the bell. The door was opened by a plump woman in a low-cut top, miniskirt, stockings and boots. Was this a brothel? I'd expected more than that. The Arab led me through a curtained doorway and down a few steps to a tiny office full of box files, record-books and video cassettes. He pulled one of the latter, in an unmarked white box, from its place near the end of a shelf. 'Rien?' I asked.

He smiled. 'Two hundred francs, please.'

That was almost all the cash I had; but I could get more from the bank in the morning. I handed over the money and hefted the box in my hands; it felt surprisingly light. I cracked it open. Nothing but a plastic syringe and a small bag of rust-coloured powder.

'What the fuck?' but even as I said that, I got the point. And even if I hadn't, I was in no mood for saying no. My guide produced a scarf, lighter and spoon from a desk drawer. It was the kind of deep spoon you only get for soup in posh restaurants. He cooked up the dose for me, then let me inject it into my left arm. Faded memories from my wild years – the post-university phase when I was trying to catch up on the student life I'd been too busy studying to discover – guided me, the way you realise when you throw up that you've learnt how to do it without choking.

There was no rush and no fade-out after the injection, just a slow bittersweet surge of clarity like black coffee loaded with sugar. Or like that moment five minutes after orgasm when your brain sends a thank-you message back to your groin. Except that if that happens when you're alone, you feel a bit cheated.

My companion watched me as I rubbed my arm and breathed deeply. My face was numb; I wondered if it was a different face. He flicked the lighter again, lit up a cigarette. I saw the passion of adolescence in the flame, and the knowledge of old age in the smoke. He smiled. 'Would you like a girl?' he said. 'On the house.' I nodded, astonished.

He took my arm and led me back through the featureless lobby, through a side door and along an unlit hallway. The door at the end was locked. When he unlocked it, a mercury strip light came on inside. My breath clouded in front of my face. It was like the freezer room in the supermarket where I'd had a Saturday job in my teens. The walls were lined with long metal shelves, and on each shelf there was a long wooden box. The icy floor was painted with a ring of what looked like cabbalistic symbols, and randomly marked with dried stains of rust. There was a smell of incense and formaldehyde.

'What kind of girl would you like?' he said. 'Virgin, whore, mistress? Blonde, redhead, skinhead? White, Asian, African? Fresh or long-preserved? Say the word and I can bring her back to life for you. All it takes is the right words, and a photograph.' He reached up to a shelf by the door and took down one of several leather-bound volumes, then flicked over a few pages. It was full of photographs of young women, cut from newspapers and magazines.

'One thing to keep in mind,' he said, as calmly as if he were discussing museum exhibits. 'There's some loss of… detail with time. Like celluloid, they start to fade. Those lovely girls from before the war, so feminine, so precious… not the same. I recommend the more recent girls. You never get good head from a skull.'

I realised the whole thing was an elaborate kind of theatre. He'd recite a formula, burn some powder, do this and that, there'd be a cloud of smoke, and a prostitute would appear from the next room in white face make-up. But the intense cold made me fear there might be more to it. I don't know whether it was disbelief or readiness to believe that made me say, 'Not this time. I'm feeling sick. Need some fresh air.' He didn't follow me back.

The young woman in the lobby gave me a bright smile before unbolting the door. I felt an overwhelming urge to touch her. But by the time she turned round the desire had passed, leaving no aftertaste. It was like I was just watching a film. 'Do come again,' she said. Then she closed her eyes and backed off with her arms crossed over her chest. I imagined her floating down a dark river on a funeral barge. Then I stepped through the narrow doorway and out into the normal world.

Worms were dropping slowly from the moon's pitted face onto the ruined landscape of the city. Isolated windows gleamed from black towers still standing amid the rubble. Wet trees folded and undulated in a wind that twisted the view. A grey cloud trailed feelers over the roofs of cars, putting out their headlights. There was no trace of colour anywhere in the scene.

I began walking frantically from street to street, trying to get back to the cinema. The rain was eroding signs and façades, leaving a series of featureless grey sets. Long, glistening trails of slime clung to the uneven pavement. A dog was pulling a half-eaten child from a waste bin. A blonde girl in a leather jacket and skirt beckoned to me from an alley; then she unzipped her jacket and ran her fingers over the broken ribs that protruded from her flesh.

Whatever her heart might cost, I couldn't afford it. I turned away and ran, gulping the petrol-tinged air. Eventually I reached a black dome that looked familiar. Could it be Sacré-Coeur? I tried to find it on my map, but the rain dissolved the words. My map was ruined and my guide was a fake. I was twenty thousand leagues under the sea.

Though it was still night, the church bells began to ring. Other bells answered them, from every direction across the city. They were cracked, waterlogged, out of tune. As I stumbled from one disfigured landmark to another, cars and taxis sped past me, splashing my legs with icy water. I glimpsed a driver pausing at an intersection. His face was puffy and dead white, with swollen eyes, like a man who'd spent his life in the cinema.

After hours of wandering, made bearable only by the cold rationality of the drug, I reached a place I recognised from films: the Cimitière de Montmartre. The gate was open. Stone steps led me down to a gap in the dark cemetery wall. Inside, granite vaults and marble angels shone in the faint moonlight. Trees wept over inscribed stone, and dense shrubbery covered up the black soil. I could still feel the drug slowing my heart, stroking my nerves; but there were no hallucinations here. Because death already lived here, there was no need for an agent to recreate it. In that moment, I think I was closer to the heart of Rien's films than I had ever been.

The slow decay of the scene allowed me to feel my own exhaustion. The magic was fading. I lay down on the surface of a family vault, my hands reading someone's epitaph, and fell asleep. I dreamt of a funeral parlour with a window display of skulls, all muttering to each other, 'We'll always have Paris.' I woke to find that the rain had stopped, and the bells were no longer ringing. A few minutes later, I realised it was daylight. The difference was purely cosmetic.

The effects of the drug had pretty much worn off. I ate a late breakfast in a Montmartre café, and walked back through the old district towards the Gare Saint-Lazare. Every street reminded me that membership of Europe is a privilege we hardly deserve. My good mood lasted me through a slow hour at Charles de Gaulle airport. They asked me if I had anything to declare; I said, 'Rien.' on the plane, I drank a glass of red wine and thought about Judith.

When I got home, early on Sunday evening, I realised at once that something had changed. The traffic noise in the house was sharper, closer at hand. I walked through to the back of the house; the larger kitchen window was broken. If the burglar alarm had worked, it hadn't made much difference. My VCR and all my videos, including the copies and blank tapes, were gone.

SEVEN

As autumn darkened into winter, I took refuge in the
normality of routine. Days at work, where the local paper
talked rubbish about terrorism in order to fortify the
national papers' rubbish about Iraq. Train journeys of
reading detective novels or staring at the charcoal-drawn
Warwickshire landscape. Evenings of sitting by the gas
fire, reading or watching videos – the insurance money
having allowed me to replace the more commercial items
of my film collection, and to add a few more classic horror
films to it. Weekends with Judith, an opportunity to lose
myself in the misshapen but breathing couple-thing we
had become. And occasionally, to feel so close to her that
my own thoughts didn't register.

Then there was politics – the familiar routine of
meetings, petitions, leafleting, demonstrations. From the
grand speeches of big-time activists to the patient anger of
local campaigners; from the raging hostility of born-again

Christians to the bored abuse of the police. The opposition to the war grew as the missiles were loaded. There was a terrible sense of unreality to the whole business. As Hitchcock said, if a gun is pulled out then by the end of the scene it has to be fired. Bush had pulled out his gun already, and it would be fired. Everything else was just filler dialogue.

In November, a series of rainstorms demolished most of the fence separating my garden from that of the empty house next door. The garden shed collapsed, as if the wind had been searching for lost property. In the house, damp began to creep down one of the partition walls and along the skirting-boards on the ground floor. I was caught between water getting in from above and water getting in from below. The growing nocturnal population of slugs and woodlice on the ground floor, once again, made me feel less than human. As if I belonged among them.

Judith spent Christmas with her family. She asked me if I'd like to come with her, but seemed relieved when I said I didn't know them well enough. I'd never been to her parents' house in Banbury, though we'd once met for lunch at a jazz café in a Leamington basement. I'd never met her two brothers. On Christmas morning, I unwrapped the presents she'd left for me: a book about the British film industry, a bottle of tequila and a CD of the new Leonard Cohen album. The latter had a small card attached with the words: *So long as I don't have to listen to it! J xx*

The last I'd heard, Cohen had gone into retirement on a mountain. The new songs – which relied heavily on Sharon Robinson's accompanying vocals – were tender and lonely. There was a sense of both distress and peace being not far away, as if the singer were somehow next door to his life. The strongest track was 'Alexandra Leaving', a haunting and dignified love song that was really about hermeneutics, the search for meanings – the ideas that cultural scholars had grappled with before they settled for the icy detachment of semiotics.

I read in the *NME* that Cohen had started taking Prozac, which had relieved him from his lifelong depression. That annoyed me. He'd struggled with despair all his life, using every possible remedy: philosophy, religion, sex, travel – and none of it had worked. Then a pill made it all go away. How could we take him seriously anymore? Then, later, I felt ashamed of my anger. Didn't the old bugger deserve some peace of mind?

I spent most of Christmas Day reading the British film book. There was a lengthy discussion of *Breaking the Waves*, the bleak religious film that Lars Von Trier had made on location in Scotland. A footnote stated: 'Some devotees of the obscure French director Jean Rien claim that he made a film called *La nuit qui brille* (at some time in the early seventies) near Stonehaven on the west coast of Scotland, in the area where an old village had crumbled into the sea. However, no trace of either the film or the village appears to exist.' I found Stonehaven on the map, close to Aberdeen.

A few days later, I tried to sell the idea of a romantic winter weekend in Scotland to a hungover Judith. I played on her regret that we hadn't had a white Christmas. 'There's bound to be snow on the ground up there. It'll be dead quiet, just the two of us. We might find the village, we might not. Doesn't really matter. We can stay in the town.' Judith agreed sleepily that that sounded nice, and went to make some coffee. I don't think she really expected me to do anything about it.

On the morning of Saturday 12th January, we caught an early train to Aberdeen. I'd bought an Ordnance Survey map of the coastal area around Stonehaven, and one bay in particular (where a couple of roads suddenly turned back from the coast) looked promising. The village must have been gone a long time for its name to have been forgotten; but surely local people would know about it. I gazed through the window at the increasingly bare landscape, and thought of Eliot's line: *The houses are all gone under the sea.*

As I'd predicted, much of northern Scotland was covered with snow. Farm houses, rocks and naked trees marred a landscape of glittering white. The sky was the blue of a Romero zombie. The train compartment was sweaty and airless; Judith and I took turns to fetch coffee and fruit juice from the buffet carriage. While Judith dozed, I tried to remember what Will Padgett had told me about *La nuit qui brille*. Perhaps the scenes of the town had been shot inland. I imagined the black sea eroding the houses like blindness.

By the time we reached Aberdeen it was dark. The mist-polished granite buildings made me think of the cemetery at Montmartre. We walked around for a few minutes, drawing the cold air into our limbs, then went back to the station and caught a local train to Stonehaven. It began to snow as the train rattled along the coast. Without stars, the only way to tell the North Sea from the night was by the sound of waves dragging gravel up and down the shore. When we reached the town, it was snowing too heavily to think of exploring further. We booked into a small hotel, ate some fresh seafood and drank some wine. The snow muffled the sounds of traffic, but not the restless murmur of the sea.

Neither of us slept well that night. Whether it was the lack of exercise, the grilled prawns or the distant crashing of waves on rocks, I'm not sure. I normally sleep well in a strange bed, which had prompted comments from Judith about my wayward youth. There was just something in the air that wouldn't let us forget how far we were from home. We made love twice – three times, if you count a failed attempt – but it didn't bring sleep. And insomnia is always a solitary experience, even if your lover can't sleep either.

In the morning, after several cups of coffee, we ventured down the treacherous cliff steps to the rocky shore. The sunlight felt like cold water on our faces. The incoming tide had washed the snow from the black shingle overnight. We walked along the shoreline, holding hands. There was no trace of ruins, no sign of a landslide, anywhere in sight. The North Sea was a vast dark slab, marked only by random scratches, its secrets buried deep inside. The hotel manager had said she didn't know about any lost village, let alone a film about it; but she'd only lived here twenty years and had grown up inland. She'd ask around at the hotel and let us know at lunchtime.

Three hours of walking left us hungry and aching, but none the wiser. The tide was still going out, so we were able to walk close to the sea and look for ruins or pieces of debris. Black seaweed danced reluctantly in the shallows. There was a faint smell of decay, but no obvious pollution. With each new bay, I felt sure we'd find traces – not of Rien's film, but of the strange history that had drawn him to the place. I wanted to see the ruins that had inspired him. But there was nothing.

Back at the hotel, the manager told us, 'There's someone you should talk to.' She led us through the tiny lobby to the restaurant, where three elderly women were sitting with shots of malt whisky. One of them was at least ninety, and so hunched she was barely lifting her glass to drink. I think she was completely blind. 'This is Rose.' I shook her hand; it was little more than bone, but there was strength in it.

Her sightless face tilted until it was almost gazing at me. 'What do ye want to know?' she asked.

'I've read there's a place near here where a village fell into the sea. A long time ago. Do you know where it is?'

Rose smiled with lips that were like soft bones. 'Aye. It's under the sea.' Behind me, Judith laughed. 'But I know where it used to be. Nearly two hundred years ago. A tidal wave flooded it, then a landslide buried the empty houses. I heard about it when I was a wean. But it isnae here.' She smiled again, more bleakly than before. 'It's by Sandhaven, forty miles north.'

In our room, Judith and I pored over the map and argued. I wanted to go there in the afternoon, but Judith was worried that we might not get back to Aberdeen in time for the last train home. We both had work on Monday. 'Your quest for this celluloid grail is taking over our lives. I think we've come far enough.' I decided to wait until we reached Aberdeen, then see how much time there was.

By daylight the North Sea coast was almost as bleak as by night. Clifftop trees were bent into crooked postures by decades of fighting the wind. The sea was a grey scroll, endlessly being wiped clean and rewritten. Dark boats fluttered on the shifting layers of water. By the time we reached Aberdeen, sleet was falling heavily. I pointed out a train to Fraserburgh on the destination board; we could walk to Sandhaven from there. But Judith wouldn't hear of it.

On the narrow inter-city train to Birmingham, we settled down with large whiskies and a major sleep debt. I was angry that we'd wasted a trip and not even stayed to find the lost village. Judith was unimpressed with my attitude. 'A romantic weekend away. You said. But were you interested in being with me? You couldn't even enjoy what was there, you were so busy searching for the fucking unknown. The village under the sea. The film that never was. It's all a substitute for something you think's been taken away from you. I'm sick of it, Martin. I'm sick of being a widow to this homemade religion of yours. You can stick the great mystery up your arse.'

I got up with the intention of fetching us both some coffee; but Judith turned and stared at the grey net curtain of rain that was flapping against the carriage window. Her action was so dismissive I picked up my bag and coat, and moved to the next carriage – which was full, so I went on to the back of the train where a few teenagers and old drunks were smoking. I sat by the window, blinking at the smoke, almost crying with fury. Someone had discarded a book of *Love Life Horoscopes*; I tore out pages at random and folded them into boats, aeroplanes, birds.

I'd been doing that for maybe twenty minutes when I heard a sound like dry thunder from outside the window. I looked up and saw a freight train, its metallic containers filled with broken stones, heading along a cross-track straight towards the last carriage. It didn't seem close enough to be a threat. But somehow it overtook us, rattling past the window, the angle narrowing until it crashed into the middle of the passenger train.

———

The papers, echoing songs the journalists had probably never heard, called it 'the border tragedy'. I was one of ninety-three people who escaped or were rescued from the twisted wreck of the 15:02 from Aberdeen. My left elbow was shattered and I had broken glass in my cheek, but I got off the train and was standing there, as if waiting for the next station announcement, when the ambulances arrived. Or so they tell me; I don't remember anything except a vague sense of having lost my own body, like an image on a cinema screen. In hospital they told me Judith was dead. In all, forty-one people died.

The freight train had come through a faulty set of points. It was running two hours late. A subsequent investigation revealed that maintenance work on the system was a year behind schedule, a consequence of the rail franchise having put the needs of its shareholders before those of its passengers.

The Health and Safety Executive charged the franchise's executive board with criminal negligence; but a judge later instructed them to drop the charges. The chairman of the franchise was quoted as saying: 'Running a business cost-effectively is not a crime. It's obscene for enemies of the private sector to make political capital out of a tragic accident.' There were eventual compensation payments that added insult to injury. If all the people killed by cost-effectiveness were killed by terrorism, the country would be in a permanent state of emergency.

Judith was cremated in Banbury. I attended with my arm in plaster. The vicar remembered her as a child. Her family neither accepted nor rejected me. They were stunned by grief. I couldn't shake off the feeling that they knew my search for Rien's films had caused the crash. Not just caused us to be on the train, but caused the freight train to hit the carriage Judith was on. My tears were hypocritical, but I still cried.

A fortnight later, I went to the last anti-war demo before the invasion began. Nearly two million people marched through London: the biggest demonstration in this country's history. But the space by my side seemed infinite. By the time I got to Hyde Park, it was literally covered with people: a sea of banners and placards. My arm was hurting badly. I felt sick and disconnected. We all knew the bombs would fall, so what was the point?

If Judith had left me, I would have coped with it. Her death didn't just break the relationship: it broke my connection to the world. I was beginning to make the transition, though I didn't know it. Walking through the streets of Birmingham in the spring, I froze every time I saw someone like Judith: similar dark hair, bone structure, jacket, blouse, hands. Every time, I felt sure the mistake was about to be corrected. I didn't mind if she'd changed her name, left the area, was living with someone else; just as long as she was alive. Every few days that happened, for months.

I gave up on the films and whatever they might have represented. Apart from work, I went out as little as possible. Yet the house, with its constant reminders of Judith, did nothing to comfort me. I slept on the right-hand side of the bed, by the wall; she always preferred being able to slip out without shifting the duvet. The decay of the house got worse, but I took no action to stop it. When I thought about the house, I thought ruin was the natural order of things. Mostly I didn't think about it. My grief was slow and cold and relentless. Sleep wasn't a retreat anymore, it was a trap. It left me floating in a station where Judith waited for train after train, but no one got out to meet her.

So a year went past. The Americans took over Iraq, but the weapons of mass destruction proved as elusive as the films of Jean Rien. In September I heard that Johnny Cash had died; it seemed like another fragment of America's conscience flaking away. I listened to 'Man in Black' endlessly through the autumn – as well as 'Small Change' by Tom Waits, a bitter song about a murder that destroyed the soul of a town. I heard something in those songs that told me where to go. But I still needed a map.

EIGHT

The clue that led me to the final phase of my search for the lost films of Jean Rien wasn't sent to me. By now, I didn't need messages. The world was changing. In late January, the last phase of winter, I was flicking hastily through the office copy of *The Independent* in my coffee break. The international news section was dominated by the Middle East, but the following report appeared at the bottom of a page:

MEXICAN TRIAL DRAWS A BLANK

The trial of an avant-garde Mexican filmmaker, Juan Nada, ended in confusion yesterday. The Mascaròn court heard that Nada's prosecution for conspiracy, arson and criminal damage could not proceed due to the deaths of key witnesses. The police say these deaths are not suspicious. Nada, 79, retired from filmmaking in 2001.

A search on the Internet yielded no further information; no other paper seemed to have reported the story, and the BBC website carried only a shortened version of the same report. I had never travelled outside Europe. What I knew about Mexico came largely from Peckinpah films, Kerouac novels, Bradbury stories and the pub joke about Pancho the bandido. None of which would be much help to me.

To get to Mexico by ship would take seven days. I didn't know how long I'd have to stay there, but I was determined not to fail this time. Which, I felt sure, meant that I wouldn't return. Whatever Rien's films were hiding couldn't be paid a visit. I asked the *Warwick View* for voluntary redundancy, and when they refused I handed in my notice. That weekend, I put my house on the market. The estate agent, a fast-talking youth in an Armani suit, had secured an offer within three days.

The next few weeks felt strangely disconnected, like a montage of stills from different films. There wasn't much daylight, but the frost on the streets created an unreal second light. It felt as though the city was scarred or diseased, shedding patches of old skin and growing new ones. I thought of Judith, and how little good I'd ever done her. The city was my prison – but I was about to escape, like a war criminal, to some kind of exile. More strongly than ever, I had the sense of time running backwards. Whatever I was about to do had already happened.

At the end of February, I arranged for most of my possessions to be taken into storage. I took what I could travel with – clothes, a few books, instant coffee. Then I left the house to the woodlice and the new owner. In a hotel room in Swansea I said goodbye to Judith, told her what I was going to do. The ghost of her disbelief made me realise how flimsy my evidence was. I smelt her perfume for a moment as we kissed goodbye.

———————

The winter sea was black and turbulent, and its salty breath could freeze the skin off your face. Waves rose and tilted like headstones in a Fulci graveyard. But the inside of the ship felt no more unstable than a hangover. There were about ninety passengers, some travelling in more luxury than others. My cabin was tiny and had a claustrophobic bunk, but I was comfortable enough. There was a passenger bar that served real ale. It was during a late-night session there that I met Eleanor.

She was a tall woman, dressed in black (casual rather than goth), with an air of being severely unimpressed. I'd seen her rebuff a young man who'd tried to chat her up at the bar, so I was quite surprised when she gave me a tired smile as our paths crossed in the doorway. 'Good evening,' she said. There was something foreign in her voice. She reminded me of the post-Velvets Nico. I'd have guessed her age to be about thirty-five.

The next time she was waiting at the bar, I joined her. The same smile, wary but conspiratorial, as if trying to establish whether I knew the secret. I asked her if she'd like a drink. 'A rum and Coke, please,' she said.

'I haven't seen you here before.' It was the third night out of Swansea. 'I was seasick.' She sipped her drink slowly, keen not to surrender her recently regained balance. We sat at one of the small half-lit tables and talked. Eleanor was Spanish, but had been living in Cardiff; presumably she'd anglicised her name. She was visiting Mexico on business. I asked her what kind of business. 'Unfinished business,' she said. I told her I was researching Mexican cinema. At that a shadow seemed to pass over her face, and I felt I ought to change the subject.

After a second round of drinks, Eleanor said, 'Well, I'd better go while I can still walk straight.' Her hand slipped onto mine. 'Let's meet tomorrow. Lunchtime, here?' The same smile, but this time it was tinged with a subtle bitterness. We agreed to meet, and she took off. I carried on drinking. If nothing else, I told myself, I'd made a friend. There was a stillness about her that appealed to me.

I hadn't thought of getting close to anyone since the train crash. After all, my relationship with Judith hadn't ended – she just wasn't there anymore. I'd felt a buried twinge of desire every time I'd walked past the massage parlour near my home in Tyseley, but I'd never stopped and rung the bell. There'd been a kind of comfort in knowing the place existed: an open door, an open pair of legs. Fantasy and deprivation always go together.

Eleanor and I got drunk together a few times during the week. She seemed to appreciate the company of someone as pessimistic as her. We exchanged bitter reflections on religion, history and the state of the world. She loved Buñuel; I told her I'd enjoyed *The Exterminating Angel*. She told me she'd seen Almodóvar at a peace demo in Barcelona, but she wasn't crazy about his films. 'Too camp, too dramatic. But at least he understands the humanity of damaged people.' She lent me a book of Lorca's poems, which I struggled through with the aid of a pocket Spanish dictionary. I remember a poem about a dead child: *muerto en la orilla, un arćangel de frio*. Dead on the bank, an archangel of frost.

We were united in our distaste for the oil baron in the White House. 'He's like the school bully whose father is the local police chief,' Eleanor said. 'He's shaking your hand in front of the teacher, then when the teacher's back is turned he's twisting your arm to make you kneel before him. Look at the eyes, always. Bush has the eyes of a man who likes to hurt.'

The air inside the ship, as well as on deck, got steadily warmer over the last three days of the voyage. You could tell the ship had been made in northern Europe: the heating was formidable, but the aircon wasn't up to much. The winter melted away, like frost on a window in sunlight. I began practising Spanish phrases on Eleanor. We were spending more and more time together, but she didn't sleep with me until the last night before docking. I think she wanted to avoid awkwardness if it went badly. She was quite insecure, and so was I.

For the last evening, I booked us a table in the ship's restaurant. We got through two bottles of wine with a meal of lobster, shallots and crusty bread. I made a mental note to myself to regret missing out on the stark Hodgson seafaring experience… in retrospect. Eleanor gripped my hand as we drank; under the table, her foot rubbed against my ankle. I couldn't tell if she was excited or fearful at the prospect of returning to Mexico. I felt a sense of completion, of being close to the end. Being in love – or in lust – made the darkness feel like home.

Over the debris of the meal, we finally talked about our reasons for travelling to Mexico. I told Eleanor about the strange black-and-white film I'd seen on video. How the idea of Rien's films had become like a religion to me. How the subject of those films was trying to cover its tracks, hide from the light. I still didn't understand what had happened in Paris, but I tried to explain it. 'For a few hours I became part of that world. His films are a way of seeing.' I'd already told her what had happened to Judith, but now I told her how I thought that was connected to Rien. Finally, I told her about the newspaper story. 'I know they're the same man.'

Eleanor nodded slowly. 'Yes, they are.'

'Are you humouring me?' The wine was making everything too clear and too blurred at the same time.

'No, I'm telling you. The thing that Juan Nada worships, the god of nothing. It killed my lover.'

Eleanor refilled our glasses while I stared at her. Then she continued her story. 'It was nine years ago, before I came to England. I was living in Madrid, working as the manager of a cinema. I liked hanging out with filmmakers, film students, actors. That whole scene. I got involved with a French actor, Philippe. He was beautiful, a fair-haired boy with a smile that burned. But he was going nowhere. Then he got this offer. To make a film for a French director, but in Mexico. The director's name was Jean Rien. Philippe had never heard of him.

'We went to Mexico together. It was a holiday for me, but Philippe said they needed extras, I could get some work. I could pass for Mexican. The film was supposed to take a fortnight. In the end, it was never finished. I suppose Rien is still making it. *La mort des témoins*, it was called. The death of the witnesses.

'Rien was filming in the desert, miles from any town. There were some ruins there. An old town where no one had lived for fifty years. Philippe and I had a trailer. He was supposed to be playing a French criminal, a robber, who was hiding in Mexico. The film didn't seem to make much sense. But we were young, it was... like a honeymoon. The heat kept us awake at night. And the sound of the wind in the ruins. We held each other and couldn't sleep. But we were not afraid at first.

'The sky was an ocean of blue. The sun was a terrible ball of flame. The rocks of the desert shone blue-green and blood-red. But Rien was filming in black and white. He was a pale-faced, quiet little man who never laughed, but was always half-smiling at some joke he never explained. Philippe said he was the kind of man who'd jerk off over a dying child. The film was some kind of allegory. A ruined town full of blind people, worshipping something they thought was an angel, but in fact it was the face of their own madness. I suppose we both thought it would be a good film. But we hated the man who was making it.

'In the film, a group of homeless people were living in the ruined city. Some disease or... influence blinded them. I was one of the extras who played most of the group. Rien made us wear patches stuck over our eyes, so we really couldn't see. Then there were the tunnels. He'd found some old burial mounds in the hills, one of the Indian tribes that died out. There were seven tunnels under the ground. Looters had taken whatever was down there. They were just dead ends. Rien wanted to film down there. At first he'd just take a few of us at a time, let us stumble around and walk into walls. It was cold down there, even when it was hot

73

above the ground. There was a smell of dust and stone and something almost rotted away.

'We knew it would end with all of us down there. The robber would be sacrificed to the god of the city. Rien talked about it like there would be a real sacrifice. He promised us drugs, peyote and acid, as well as all the booze we could drink before the scene was shot. I was frightened it would get out of control. Some of the men, the actors and extras, had tried to get their hands on me. I was frightened of what they might do in the tunnels. Philippe was worried about that, but something else frightened him even more. He'd been down there without eye patches. I asked him what he'd seen, but he said there was nothing.

'The last night before we were going to film the sacrifice, Philippe held me like a child holding his mother. He said he was afraid Rien might blow up the tunnels. "There's nothing he won't do to make his film." I knew he was afraid of something else, but I didn't know what. Philippe made love to me until I was tired. I fell asleep next to him. When I woke up in the morning, he was gone.

'There was no sign of him in the ruins. No cart was missing, so he hadn't gone back to Laredo. Rien and his production team said he must have wandered off. They wanted to film the big scene anyway. But I insisted we search the tunnels. It was the first time I'd been down there and able to see.' Eleanor paused. 'We found him in the tunnels.' She closed her eyes; I gripped her hand. 'In all seven tunnels. I had to gather him. A harvest of Philippe. He was so cold.'

'I'm sorry,' I said uselessly.

'The police were called. But there were no answers. The film was never finished. Nobody was paid. I spent all the money I had on his burial. I couldn't go back home. For months I worked in bars and shops. Eventually I went to Europe, ended up in Wales. Another land of the dead.' Eleanor laughed quietly. 'I tried to get over it, start a new life. But you don't get over something like that. It drags you down.'

'Are you going there to find out what happened to him?'

'There's nothing to find. The police were just going through the motions. He was a foreigner, what did they care? Maybe I'll see Rien again, or whatever he calls himself. But what will he tell me? The truth makes no difference. I'm going back to be where he is.'

By now, we'd finished the wine and drunk some coffee. It was time to pay the bill. I wanted to ask Eleanor what part I could play in her future. But the question sounded selfish, even petulant, in my mind. She seemed to understand, because she gripped my hand and said, 'It's hard to travel alone.' We went on to the bar and stood, swaying slightly, drinking brandy. She kissed me. I took her hand and we walked from the bar, down a few steps, and along a corridor to my cabin.

I watched her undress by the light of a small oil-lamp. Her body seemed both strong and fragile. Her long hair rippled over her amber skin. The flickering of the lamp marked her body with flecks of darkness, unstable shadows that made her seem incomplete. She was beautiful, and I had felt hunger in her kiss. Yet somehow, I didn't feel the rush of excitement I usually felt with a new lover. The sense of danger, of transgression, was missing. Instead, I felt a deeper, less simple need to be with her. Could it be that, at the age of forty-one, I was finally becoming an adult? Then she reached for me, and all such thoughts disappeared as we moved together in the smoky light.

The bunk wasn't wide enough for two, so we spread the blankets on the floor. It was a warm night. At some point before dawn, I fell into a deep narcotised sleep. We awoke in the morning, decided to skip breakfast, and kept the curtain drawn over the porthole. We were half awake, starting to make love for the fourth or fifth time, when the engine shuddered and became still. We lay in the new silence, breathless. The ship had docked in the bay of Veracruz.

NINE

Within a couple of hours, we were standing in the town square. We'd booked into a small hotel, then walked along the promenade and visited the market. Masks and dolls were sold alongside fruit, leather goods and cheap videos. The streets were grey, baked dry; the mosaic of architectural styles was evidence of recurrent warfare and rebuilding. In the dense, grainy sunlight, the shadows looked as real as walls. Somehow, without discussing it, we had decided to stay together. Eleanor's quiet presence beside me, her familiarity with the place, gave me such an unfamiliar sense of belonging that it was a while before I noticed what was wrong. Grey adobe walls; black shadows; a shimmering white sky. I couldn't see any colours.

Eleanor was subdued. She'd made a number of phone calls from our hotel room, and now I realised she was looking for something. Lack of sleep made both of us slow and uncoordinated. She led me through a festering maze of backstreets that reminded me of my drug-induced version of Paris. Some of the little shacks appeared to have been moulded by hand from wet clay. At last, she bought a tiny foil-wrapped package from a blind man who was standing casually outside his house. When we got back to the hotel, she cooked up a dose of fine greyish powder and injected us both. The needle stung, but within minutes the pain had faded into a sleepwalking blankness. I saw every detail clearly, but felt nothing. Eleanor's calves and ankles were pitted with tiny dark sores. She said they were insect bites.

Over the next couple of days, we took a lot of heroin together. This was going a long way beyond the experiments of my younger days. But I accepted it because I believed it would take us closer to Rien. It was part of the journey I'd spent my life preparing for. And as in Paris, it changed my sense of time. Our lovemaking became protracted, never brought to a conclusion. A kiss on a train platform or a touch of hands in the street had as much intensity as full sex a few hours later, and was not distinct from it. Our love affair became a montage.

We travelled across the desert realm of southern Mexico on a series of rattling trains. The architecture drifting past the train windows regressed to beat-up towns, stark villages of adobe huts, sand-blasted Aztec ruins. It was hard to talk over the percussion of the bare wheels. At night, the wind howled in ravines, bare trees and ruined buildings. I began to wish we'd gone to Ibiza. Eleanor was silent most of the time. I could smell decay on her skin, taste it in her mouth.

At Oaxaca, we made a detour to find more smack. Eleanor had got hold of a name in a nearby town, so we walked several miles across the desert to pick up the gear at a run-down hotel. We booked a room to shoot up in the grainy afternoon light. Despite the heat, something about the bare walls and the narrow bed made me shiver. I wondered if someone had been killed in here and a kind of shock remained, too weak and sick to be called a ghost. We injected each other, a protracted and oddly sexual act that made me feel closer to Eleanor, despite the dark lesions I could see covering more and more of her legs and torso. They weren't insect bites, but they weren't needle tracks either. They were like something inside breaking through.

Afterwards, we had a few drinks in the hotel bar. A cluster of salesmen were drinking bottled beer and sneering into their mobile phones. On the train, Eleanor had encouraged me to try and speak Spanish; but here, I let her do most of the talking. It wasn't wise to be an obvious foreigner. We bought a half-bottle of mescal. Its greasy taste dried out my mouth. As I poured the last measures into our glasses, I saw the worm begin to writhe.

We finally arrived at Mascaròn late in the afternoon. The setting sun was dissolving the view. As the train drew into the battered-looking station, a dog barked from the platform. When we dragged our suitcases from the train, we saw the dog was chained to a wooden pillar. It was thin and black, and it jerked from side to side so fast that it appeared to have more than one head. Eleanor and I were the only people getting off the train. The dog stopped barking to watch us pass, as if it had been told we were coming.

I wanted to track down Juan Nada, but Eleanor said there was no point. 'He won't be here. We need to find the ruins and wait for him there.' Needless to say, there was no transport that would get us to what we were looking for.

Even Eleanor had only a vague sense of the direction, and she refused to ask any of the local people. 'They won't tell us. They don't go there.' I wondered if her unease at the quiet town was connected to the number of people we saw wearing some kind of monkish costume, their faces painted or masked an expressionless white. I asked her if a festival was going on. 'There always is,' she said.

We bought some food and water, and set off across the desert as night fell. It would be cooler than by day, and there was a full moon. Eleanor told me about her childhood in Madrid, in the early years of post-Franco Spain. How the cinema had seemed to her a place of magic, where hardship and boredom gave way to the unknown and to 'things that could never be, but seemed more true than things that were'. She had shaken off her religious faith in her teens; but she had never lost the need to believe in a world beyond this one. 'Then I met Juan Nada. And he destroyed my belief. He's not a sceptic. He's a believer. But what he believes in is not a different world. It's just nothing.'

'What does he look like?' I asked, wondering if I had actually met him in Paris.

'Like a monk. Bald, pale, dressed in a robe. Always doing this with his hands.' She made a wringing gesture. 'Like those people in Mascaròn. That's why they look like that. To be the same as him.'

We walked on in silence. There were few landmarks: the odd abandoned building or rusting car, occasionally the skeleton of a horse. Around midnight, we paused to shoot up and slept for a few hours. We woke before dawn, with the moon down, and held each other without moving. The wind made a strange hollow sound, like the land crying.

'It's the tunnels underground,' Eleanor said. 'Down there, the moon is still bright.'

The morning felt cooler than the previous day. We opened our food pack, but the contents had started to go off: the pasties tasted bitter, and the fruit was slimy. Even the water had a metallic edge to it. I couldn't feel the heat of the sun, and wasn't surprised when it clouded over and the sky became a sullen grey. But Eleanor frowned. 'This isn't the season for rain,' she said. 'Climate change, I suppose.' By late morning, the ruins were still nowhere in sight. The sky was livid with darkness. But we kept going. Even moving in the wrong direction was better than staying in one place.

At last we came to a rocky peak from which we could look down onto the barren landscape of ravines and arroyos that spread for miles around us. On the horizon, and nearly in the direction we'd been travelling in, I could just make out a few scattered buildings. They did not look inhabited. The clouds shifted, and a mist of weak sunlight shimmered around the ruins. The sun was no brighter than the moon, and had the same blemishes on its surface. Then it began to rain.

Within seconds it was coming down heavily, like soft grey veils folding onto the ground. The rain felt warmer than the air, as if it was bringing down the heat the clouds had screened off. The ground blackened, then began to stream and dissolve. I stared at the distant ruins, no longer visible in the jittering downpour. Then I felt Eleanor's hand on my arm; her nails gripped my skin. 'Hold me, Martin,' she said. I turned to face her. In the rain, her features were blurred.

There was nowhere to shelter. We fell to our knees, kissing frantically. My hands traced the outline of her body through her soaked dress. She laughed and said,

'I know you think I'm unstable.' The cavities in her face were spreading, the skin giving way like old crêpe paper. Her eyes were dull. I kissed her again, but there were no lips to her mouth, and even the teeth were coming loose. 'Hold me,' she tried to repeat. Only her clothes, and my arms, were keeping her together as the bones worked free of tissue and the rain corroded her blackening skin. I ran a hand through her dark hair, felt it pull away from her skull. In the last moments, she pressed what was left of her face to my ear and moaned, 'Juan, Juan...'

'I'm not one,' I said. 'I'm nothing.' Then I was holding a black dress full of bones, and the skin my hands had touched was being washed away into the desert mud. The rain pounded and ripped through the air like a drum solo at a festival. All around me, the ground was indistinguishable from the sky. I dropped my rucksack and tried to stand up.

Somehow the mud supported me, as long as I didn't stand still. I tried to remember the direction of the ruins, and began to walk.

———————

That's my last clear memory of the desert. I came round in the hospital in Mascaròn, after what must have been days of walking aimlessly, with rainwater to drink but without food. Apparently, someone had found me lying in the street. I was three days in hospital, weak and feverish. The cash in my wallet just about paid for my care; I had to sell my watch to buy a train ticket back to the coast. As the effects of heroin use wore off, I became even less sure what had happened.

But I think I found the ruins. Or rather, they found me. I remember walls of decaying brick, roads pitted with unstable holes too deep to fill. Black trees like electricity pylons, their branches worn away by the blowing sand. A lake clogged up with metallic cinders, unreflecting black on reflecting black. Crows flapping overhead like scraps of burnt plastic. And everywhere, the cold smell of decay. Wherever I walked I could hear some kind of echo, like a train going past under my feet. It wasn't like the old Mexican towns I had seen. It was more like the ruins of a modern city. I saw no people there, alive or dead.

I worked my way back to Europe, but couldn't go home. There was nothing to go back to. For the last few months I've drifted from city to city, heading nowhere in particular. I feel the need to keep searching, though I don't know what I'm searching for. Wherever I go, I'm aware of the burnt world waiting just beyond this one. The shadow behind the screen. Every night, I feel I'm about to walk into it. Perhaps it's the future we will share. Our garden of ashes. Or perhaps it's the world we've already made, but can't face.

After all, we've already suppressed its image. It wasn't the subject of the films trying to hide itself, it was us trying to bury it. Eleanor was right: to understand the cinema of Jean Rien is to give up your illusions. That's why the films seemed unreal and elusive. As anyone who's lived long enough will tell you, the human mind can only take so much reality before it shuts down. Ghosts are a form of censorship. We block out the night with ghosts, because the darkness is worse.

I don't know how I got here. Do any of us? I was

unaware, negligent, and that was enough to stamp my passport. Yet the people I've loved seem more real in my life than anyone I meet, and certainly more real than myself. Sometimes I glimpse the face of Jean Rien in the crowd, a face like a skull, and think he's still trying to tell me something.

Perhaps it's this: if the truth of our lives is nothing, then the only reality is the one we bring to life. After all, our cities – our tower blocks, our bridges, our streets – are human constructs. They didn't come from nature. Why should our dreams, desires and fears be any different? Whatever we make in our lives – love, violence, hope or betrayal – is the only reality that won't fall down overnight.

ACKNOWLEDGEMENTS

This story takes its core idea from 'The Vanishing Life and Films of Emmanuel Escobada', which appeared anonymously in *Nemonymous* 2 and whose author has chosen to remain nameless, but has kindly given permission for the story to be developed in the present work. Thanks are due to him or her.

Thanks are also due to John Wells, whose unpublished poem 'Views of a Black Earth' is quoted in this story.

Finally, thanks are due to the following for help, support, encouragement and strange films: Peter and Nicky Crowther, Conrad Williams, Nicholas Royle, Ella Lane, John Howard, Steve and Ann Green, Ray Holloway, Simon Bestwick, Des Lewis, Mick Scully, Christina Morris, Gul Davis, Mat Joiner, Cinephilia.

Photo by Nicholas Royle

Joel Lane was the author of two novels, *From Blue to Black* and *The Blue Mask*; several short story collections, *The Earth Wire*, *The Lost District*, *The Terrible Changes*, *Do Not Pass Go*, *Where Furnaces Burn*, *The Anniversary of Never* and *Scar City*; a novella, *The Witnesses Are Gone*; and four volumes of poetry, *The Edge of the Screen*, *Trouble in the Heartland*, *The Autumn Myth* and *Instinct*. He edited three anthologies of short stories, *Birmingham Noir* (with Steve Bishop), *Beneath the Ground* and *Never Again* (with Allyson Bird). He won an Eric Gregory Award, two British Fantasy Awards and a World Fantasy Award. Born in Exeter in 1963, he lived most of his life in Birmingham, where he died in 2013.

Influx Press is an independent publisher based in London, committed to publishing innovative and challenging literature from across the UK and beyond.

Lifetime supporters: Bob West and Barbara Richards

www.influxpress.com
@Influxpress